LION'S LAIR

A ZODIAC SHIFTER PARANORMAL ROMANCE: LEO

ANN GIMPEL

Edited by
KATE RICHARDS

CONTENTS

LION'S LAIR

A ZODIAC SHIFTER PARANORMAL
ROMANCE: LEO

Wylde Magick, Book Two
By
Ann Gimpel

Copyright Page

Strong and self-assured, Jeremiah is the closest thing his mage kinfolk have to an alpha. He takes his responsibilities seriously, which hasn't left time for much of anything, and it's about to get worse. Mages are in trouble. A few signed on with vampires, causing human deaths. Because of them, all mages are being smeared with the traitor brush.

Renee's eagle bondmate jerks her awake one night with the terse message a cave lion, one of the most ancient of the animals, has bonded. According to the bird, they have to drop everything and go to Colorado. Reluctant to weave the fabric of lies she'll need to cover her absence, she finally gives in.

She's horrified to discover the lion bonded with a man who used to be a mage. A mage. The rogues who joined up with vampires. She wants to hate Jeremiah, but it's a tough sell. Not only is he gorgeous, he's smart and kind and funny. None of it matters, though, because he doesn't like her, either.

Are the hurdles too high? Or is a shifter's mate truly in the stars?

In astrology-speak, Leo is a fixed fire sign, and those born under it are natural leaders. Dramatic, creative, self-confident, and dominant, they're extremely difficult to resist. When things go well, they're able to achieve anything they want to. They often have many friends for they are generous and loyal.

On the flip side, Leo hates being ignored, facing difficult realities, and not being treated like a king or queen. They are perfectly capable of running roughshod over those who they feel have slighted them and can be quite temperamental.

CHAPTER 1

*A*ngry honking snapped Jeremiah Fuller back to the present. He goosed the gas, only to be bombarded by more irritated honks and the screech of brakes.

"Goddammit!" he sputtered and pounded a fist into the steering wheel of his classic 1965 Corvette Stingray. He loved the shiny black car, had spent hundreds of hours restoring it to pristine condition. That he'd nearly sacrificed a fender, or goddess forbid his entire front end, to a stupid accident disgusted him.

He had to pull it together and shelve his problem *du jour* for now. No more excuses.

Peering left, right, and over both shoulders to make certain it was safe, he drove away from the four-way stop that had almost been his undoing. Rather than turning right at the next corner—his normal route home—he kept on driving straight.

He wasn't fit company for the mages he lived with, not until he sorted through the vision that had dogged him ever since his close call luring vampires to their deaths. He'd ingested a powerful toxin on the reluctant advice of Raul, their group's healer.

Raul hadn't wanted to compound the poison, let alone give it to him, but Jeremiah outranked him. He'd demanded a substance that would keep him alive long enough to mete out maximum damage to a vampire horde—presuming he could induce them to feed from him. He hadn't worried about the last part. Enticing vamps was never much of a feat since they weren't known for turning down any neck that swung their way.

Jeremiah had fully expected to die. The lead-and-silver-based poison would kill him too, but not as fast as it destroyed the vampires. He'd said his goodbyes and come to terms with his decision. If he dissuaded even a handful of mages from joining ranks with vampires, it would be worth it. He'd been on his way out, hovering at the brink of crossing the veil, when a shifter medicine man cast magic of his own to save him.

That had been two weeks ago. At first, the shifters had been horrified by what they considered a foolhardy move on his part. They'd gotten over that, though. He wasn't privy to their internal discussions, but he would have bet his last spell that Sarai Lurie, a wolf shifter, had turned the tide in his favor.

He cranked down a window and savored the wind scouring his overheated face. Mages and shifters had a rocky history. If you were to ask a shifter, they'd describe those like him as failed shifters, and the sad truth was many mages viewed themselves the same way.

Jeremiah tightened his grip on the wheel. It was a shame. Mage power was different from shifter magic in subtle and not-so-subtle ways. True, they couldn't entice an animal to bond with them, but they had other skills shifters lacked, like the ability to coax all living things to shine brightly. Mages were exceptional gardeners and ranchers and farmers. They channeled power from the gods to ensure crops would yield bounty, and animals would bear sturdy young. Mages were also philosophers and scholars, two talents many shifters lacked patience for.

His particular skill was communicating with trees, bushes, and birds. Though he didn't need to work because he'd amassed a fortune over his lifetime—and was prudent when it came to spending—he occasionally hired out to zoos and animal sanctuaries when they had uncooperative residents that preyed on other critters. He had a stellar reputation. Zookeepers were awed by his ability, but only because they had no idea he used magic to whip their recalcitrant charges into line.

Since he was used to dealing with stubborn, independent animals and birds, luring the vamps to feed from him had been even easier than he'd anticipated. Certainly simpler than earning a hawk's trust, but then raptors were notorious loners.

He turned hard right, taking the road to Gore Pass, but turning off miles before he crested the ten-thousand-foot crossing point along the spine of the Rocky Mountains. A series of dirt roads grew progressively worse until he left other cars behind. The low-slung Chevy finally balked as the road deteriorated to four-wheel-drive terrain. He parked, intent on covering the last couple of miles on foot. An icy wind buffeted him, and he zipped his jacket to the chin.

Moving at a lope across long-since-abandoned mining roads offered thinking time. Normally, he wasn't an overthink-things kind of guy, but ever since Ronnie, an eagle shifter, had called him back from death's door, he'd had unusual dreams. It wouldn't be so worrisome if they hadn't invaded his non-sleep time as well—

"Bullshit!" The harsh epithet forced him to face facts. He was blowing smoke, pure and simple. If he had any chance of sorting this out, he had to stop indulging in how he wanted things to be and admit the truth.

The visions were eerily weird, no matter when they showed up.

He reached the entrance to an abandoned copper mine and ducked inside. He'd discovered this spot years before. It shielded him and his magic nicely, as well as hosting several pairs of nesting raptors. They'd picked it because it sheltered their young from predators.

He'd picked it for its solitude. Another plus was no one knew about it. He sent magic zinging wide, sampling the mineshaft. The only presence he sensed was residual energy from his last visit a few months back.

Two of the hawks fluttered down from perches high above his head. One landed on his shoulder, the other on the ground in front of him. He greeted them in their language, assuring them he meant no harm. It seemed to satisfy them because they took to the air, exiting the cave amid a swoosh of wings and harsh cawing.

Black feathers floated to the ground.

Jeremiah smiled and scooped one up. Birds were magical in their own right. If he'd been a shifter, he'd have wanted to be a hawk or an eagle or one of the seabirds like cormorants, or even an albatross.

A roar filled his chest, blasting out of his mouth. He couldn't have held it in if he tried. The sound shocked him, but his lack of control over his vocal cords was downright terrifying.

Reality smashed into him like a runaway bus. The lion was back. The same one who'd battered its way through every single dream he'd had since Ronnie saved his life. At first, he thought he'd absorbed bits of residual shifter magic, that the odd visitations would fade.

They'd grown worse.

Much worse.

The lion was different enough from the commonplace variety on television nature shows, he'd Googled it. And come up with a cave lion, a prehistoric beast that had been extinct for thousands of years. Seeing the information march across his display reassured him he was caught up in some weird magical hallucination, courtesy of the eagle shifter's ministrations. Cave lions didn't exist anymore, which meant the one hounding him didn't, either.

He'd done a fine job ignoring the lion's visitations after that.

Until the goddamned, pushy creature entered his consciousness while he sat idling at that four-way stop on the outskirts of Glenwood Springs. Normally, he didn't travel quite so far west, but he was helping Niall, a jaguar shifter, pack up his house so he could move in with his mate, Sarai, at her uncle's ranch north of Denver.

Shifters were banding together. So were mages. It wasn't safe to live alone anymore. Not until they got a better handle on the foul magic running amok.

Everyone was worried about vampires. After centuries of traveling miles beneath the radar, they'd teamed up with a pack of disconsolate mages, borrowing liberally from their power. The combination was potent enough to wreak havoc. At least a dozen humans had died as a result of mages selling their skills to the highest bidder.

In this case, vampires.

Jeremiah cringed. He'd wanted to craft an excuse for his kin, but their role in the vampires' carnage was incontrovertible. It was why he'd been willing to sacrifice himself to teach them a lesson: that other mages wouldn't take their treachery lying down.

He exhaled sharply. He was stalling, coming up with diversions so he didn't have to make sense of the cave lion—the one who'd just borrowed his lungs and vocal cords to yowl. He forced his mind back to earlier that day, determined to sort through what happened.

They'd packed as much as they could fit into Sarai's uncle's old farm truck,

and he'd been on his way back to his home in

Silverthorne when the lion hijacked his mind—again. Rather than avoiding it, he'd taken a good, hard look at the beast for the first time. Keen golden eyes glared back. So did four-inch fangs and a shaggy, tawny mane. If the representation in his mind's eye was at all accurate, the beast was even larger than he'd thought. At least four feet at the shoulder, and maybe six or seven from snout to rump.

Another roar, louder than the last, ripped from him. Birds tore out of the old mine, squawking their ire and pecking at his unprotected head as they flew past. He didn't blame them.

Jeremiah stood tall, squaring his shoulders. "Who are you?" he demanded, proud his voice didn't tremble. "Tell me what you want."

For long moments, nothing happened. The odd pressure in his chest and lungs loosened. He was close to deciding the whole thing was exactly what he'd suspected, a nexus where shifter magic was doing battle with his brand of power, when searing heat started in the soles of his feet, moving upward in an inexorable tide of pain. Pins and needles ceded to knives. The wounds the eagle shifter had carved reopened, wetting his sides with bloody fluid.

He threw wards around himself, but the pain increased by a factor of a hundred until he felt like the skin was being flayed from his bones.

"Do not fight me!" blasted through his mind.

"Who are you?" Jeremiah shouted, but his mouth didn't work right, and the words came out garbled. He dropped his warding because he hurt so much he couldn't hang onto the magic.

An anguished screech shot from his mouth, followed by two more. He wasn't a coward but traveling through the nine circles of Hell couldn't hurt this much. White-hot blasts seared him from all sides.

Panting, gasping, he took a breath into lungs that had forgotten how to cooperate. The world smelled different, each scent individual and intense. It was as if he'd never smelled anything before, and he sucked air hungrily, sampling the rich variety. Who would have guessed rocks had a smell? Or that different types of bird shit each had their own tang?

The pain receded. At first, he thought it was because he had something else to focus on, but it really was lessening.

A strident rip from his jacket, and then another from his shirt, forced reluctant understanding. A glance downward solidified his knowledge. He was shifting—into the lion. Never mind it was impossible. It was happening anyway. Exultation did battle with fear.

"Wait." He switched to telepathy and fought with

limbs that were half human, half feline to divest himself of what was left of his clothes.

He saved his trousers but did a less effective job with his shirt. His jacket had already split down the back. All through his struggles, the realization he wasn't human any longer rocketed through him, heady as a rare vintage wine.

I'm shifting. I'm shifting. I'm shifting.

The words repeated like a tape loop obliterating everything else.

"So you want to be a bird, do you?" The lion's words were lined with derision. *"I was going to give you more time, but your bird fixation was so egregious I couldn't let it slide."*

Jeremiah was too overcome to craft an answer. The cavalcade of smells intensified. His vision changed, the visual field wider and deeper, but with less fine detail. Bones stretched and reformed. Fur sprouted, covering bare skin.

He'd frozen in place once his battles with his clothing ended. What was left of the pain ceased abruptly, and he forced one paw forward, followed by another. He swished his tail, liked how it felt, and did it again. Before he knew it, he'd bounded to the end of the main cavern and back again, the movement easy, effortless.

He sat back on his haunches and launched himself

upward in an experimental leap that carried him fifteen feet into the air. This time the roar that shook the old mineshaft was all him. A low, rumbling purr followed.

Before he got too carried away, he stopped moving. *"Why?"* he asked. *"Was it the eagle shifter's healing?"*

"Yes and no."

"You have to say more than that. I want to understand how it is that I, a mage, am now a shifter."

"It's the same strain of magic," the lion began.

"No, it's not," Jeremiah broke in.

Familiar pressure erupted into a roar. *"If you know so much, little mage, why ask me?"*

It was a reasonable question. *"Sorry. I know less than nothing about being part of a shifter bond. And I need to know everything."*

"My answers will not satisfy you. Mage power was primary. Shifters were an offshoot. Long ago, both branches of that magical tree could shift. I have no idea if the eagle's ministrations eliminated a blockage, but I was called from the animals' world. Your energy is a match for my own. It is how our bond forms."

Jeremiah waited, but the lion fell silent. *"Surely there's more,"* he prodded.

"No. Nothing more. See? I told you my reply would be less than satisfactory."

"It's not that. Not exactly. If what you say is true—"

Another roar, deafening and nourishing at the same time. "*I always speak the truth. To suggest otherwise demeans our bond.*"

If Jeremiah had been in his human body, he'd have cast a sidelong glance at his new partner. "*Sorry. It's a lot to wrap my mind around. Do you mean that any mage can become a shifter?*"

A slithering hiss sounding like an angry teakettle made his jowls vibrate.

"*Don't be so literal. Every mage isn't on the verge of becoming a shifter. That would be impossible. What? Do you believe an inexhaustible supply of bond animals exists?*"

"*I have no idea what to believe.*" This time the hiss was pure Jeremiah. "*Look. I was raised a mage. I understand mage magic. I never studied anything about being a shifter. Why would I have?*"

"*Show some respect.*"

Jeremiah tossed his head back, liking the way his lush mane fell around his shoulders. "*I would request the same. Most shifters find their animals when they're what? Ten? Twelve? I've been a mage for over three hundred years.*" He inhaled, trying not to get sidetracked by the luxuriant variety of scents. "*If there's some trick, or some clue, I would tell my kinfolk so maybe some of them might—*"

"*We decide. Not you.*"

Jeremiah thought about it. *"For shifters as well?"*

"Of course. Not every shifter ends up bonded."

He tried a different tack. *"When I return to my kinsmen, may I tell them about you?"*

"I would be offended if you kept me a secret."

"When I tell them, they'll want a bond animal too."

The lion hooted and howled. *"Wanting and having are not the same. Enough talk. Let us run. And hunt. Dusk is nigh, and game plentiful beyond our cave."*

WHEN JEREMIAH PICKED his way back to his car around midnight, his mind and heart were filled with wonder. And his belly was full of a tender, young buck. He'd tried to engage the lion in further dialog, but without success. He'd never understood the relationship between shifters and their animals, but apparently the bond wasn't built on conversation.

He nosed the Corvette back onto the highway and turned east. He'd take the pass route. It was shorter than backtracking to I-70. Sensation ebbed and flowed within his chest, sometimes oozing out in a purr, sometimes in a muted—or not so muted—roar.

After another lusty roar blatted through the passenger compartment, he dug his phone out of the console and dialed Niall's number. The jaguar shifter might be sleeping, but Jeremiah bet not. He needed a CliffsNotes version of how to control his animal side. Roaring in the middle of downtown Silverthorne would get him tossed in the drunk tank—or the local looney bin.

He could kick the problem around with other mages, but nothing like culling knowledge directly from the horse's—or jaguar's—mouth.

He broke a few laws by not switching the phone to Bluetooth, but it was late. The odds of a not-so-friendly cop apprehending him were slim. He waited through three rings before Niall picked up.

"Jer? What the fuck, buddy? It's like one in the morning."

"You don't sound the least bit sleepy," Jeremiah observed snidely. "I do apologize for interrupting you and Sarai, though. Wouldn't have, but this is important."

"What's important?" The phone made a few clicking sounds.

"Hi, Jer. Sarai here. What's going on? Apologies for my mate."

Niall growled, sounding like the cat he turned into.

Much to Jeremiah's dismay, he growled back.

"What was that?" Niall demanded.

"Where are you?" Sarai chimed in. "What's up? Do you need us?"

Jeremiah ground his teeth. "I'm in my car. I have a problem—" The rest of his sentence was obliterated by the lion, who apparently resented the hell out of being labelled a problem.

"Listen up." Niall's tone was all business. "Do not turn your phone off. Pull to a shoulder. I'll find you."

"I don't need to be rescued," Jeremiah blurted. "I—I'm a shifter now. I have no idea how it happened, or what to do about it"—another roar, louder this time—"but I need information. For starters, how do I control it?"

More roars blatted from him. He was on the eastern side of Gore Pass and pulled off onto a side road, killing both lights and engine. He wasn't at all certain how safe it was to keep driving with a rampaging lion on the loose. One who could force a shift exactly like it had in the cave.

"What?" Sarai shrieked.

"You heard him," Niall cut in.

"Yeah, but how could something like that happen?" Sarai was back.

"Can we sort the fine points out later?" Jeremiah spoke over both of them. "How do I make peace with my, er, bondmate? Everything I do pisses it off, and then it roars. I'm afraid I may end up shifting inside my car, which would be a disaster. The lion won't fit."

"Oooh, a lion," Sarai purred, followed by, "What

sign are you? You'd almost have to be born under Leo—"

"Which lion?" Niall spoke over his mate. "I may know it."

Jeremiah pinched the bridge of his nose between his thumb and forefinger. So far, these two weren't any help at all. "Focus. Please. What's the first thing you learned after your animal picked you?"

"We pick each other," Sarai said. "We dream them when we're young, get to know them. By the time we finally shift, they're like an old friend."

"Not exactly what my lion said," Jeremiah muttered.

"Ohohoho." Niall stretched the single word out until it had a dozen syllables.

"What exactly does that mean?" Jeremiah loosened his death grip on the steering wheel, but his stomach twisted into a hard knot.

"You're incredibly lucky," Sarai spoke up. "One of the old ones selected you. It's a fantastic honor, and I can't wait to meet it. Give me your birthdate and time, so I can pull your chart together."

"Save the astrology for later." Niall shushed his mate and aimed his next words at Jeremiah. "First off, thank the lion for choosing you. Heartfelt thanks. If you can gin up a gush—and it's genuine—do it."

"But of course, you already did that, right?" Sarai broke in.

"Um, no. I didn't, I'm afraid. This whole thing caught me unaware. I'm sure there's protocol, but it's not something taught to mages..." He was babbling, but he had a tough time stopping the word salad spewing from his mouth.

"Never mind. It will be all right," Sarai said, adding, "It will, won't it?" directed at Niall.

"Probably." Niall's words were gruff. "I've never known anyone who bonded at Jer's age."

"Doesn't make it impossible," Sarai argued, "but I'm standing by with the tarot and crystals and my offer to assemble his chart."

"I'm still here." Jeremiah could have throttled both of them. "Don't dissect me like some oddball object."

Breath whistled through Niall's teeth. "We're going to hang up. Thank the lion for choosing you. It should help smooth the waters, so long as you're sincere about it. Never underestimate the animals. They're wise in atavistic ways."

"And they read your thoughts," Sarai tossed in. "You can't ever hide anything from them."

"So it's best if I'm honest, right?" Jeremiah hunted for corroboration.

"Depends where honest takes you," Niall said

bluntly. "If you swung by Stephan's ranch, we could approach your bondmate together."

Stephan was Sarai's uncle, who lived on a ranch north of Denver. Jeremiah had a lot of respect for the mountain lion shifter who'd just lost his mate to vampires. "Thanks for the offer," he replied, "but it's too far for tonight. I'm still an hour from home as it is."

"You could visit tomorrow," Sarai said.

"Or meet us back in Glenwood to finish clearing out the rest of my house," Niall cut in.

"You are such a self-serving oaf," Sarai muttered.

"Sure and I'm not," Niall protested, his Irish brogue thicker than usual. "It would kill two birds with one stone. We could provide a crash course in shifterdom while he—"

"I'll get back to you in the morning." Jeremiah tapped the end call button and slumped against the leather upholstery. Maybe he shouldn't have disconnected so abruptly, but he didn't have the energy to listen to Niall and Sarai squabble about the best way to approach things. Besides, the lion was his bondmate, not theirs. This was one problem he needed to approach alone.

He dug deep, accessing memories he hadn't dragged out in many hundreds of years.

Once his thoughts were as organized as he could manage, he said, "I'm not sure how to talk with you, but according to Sarai, you can read my mind. If that's so, then you know I longed to bond with an animal when I was a child. What young magic-wielder wouldn't?

"Those older and wiser assured me every fledgling mage wanted an animal bondmate, and that I'd get over my yearning given time. They also told me accepting the magic the goddess had given me would go a long way toward easing the sting of not being a shifter.

"I took them seriously and did my damnedest to embrace my mage ability. I grew powerful in my magic, one of the strongest of my kind. And I was grateful for my linkage to plants and birds."

A roar filled the car, probably his cat's annoyance he'd brought up anything avian. Undaunted, he soldiered on.

"Just because I never expected to be a shifter doesn't mean I don't appreciate the miracle of you joining your nature with mine. I'm deeply pleased and more than a little overwhelmed. You're amazing, probably far more than I deserve. I will do whatever it takes to be worthy of you selecting me."

More words tumbled through his tired brain, but he stopped there. He wouldn't grovel. Any partnership worth its salt was driven by mutual respect. The lion had chosen him for his strength, not his weakness.

Jeremiah waited. When a low, rumbling purr filled

his chest and found its way out his mouth, he took it as a good sign and started the car. Miles clipped by. After ten, he felt hopeful. After twenty-five with no roars and not the slightest indication shifting was imminent, he was confident he'd hit the right note.

He had half an hour before he'd be home and wanted to use the time well.

"Since we're a team now, and I'm fighting vampires, I bet you have ideas to help vanquish those bastards."

"I thought you'd never ask." Another purr warmed him. *"First, a little history is in order…"*

$\mathcal{A}$ staunch shriek from her eagle ripped Renee Jamison from an uneasy sleep. Censure crowded the back of her throat, hot words that died before crossing her lips. She loved her bondmate, but she hadn't slept worth a shit for the last two weeks. Tonight had been an exception—because she was dead on her feet—and she'd been deeply asleep when the bird woke her.

Her head pounded, and her eyes felt gritty and sandpapery. "What?" She slurred the word as she clawed her way back from an X-rated dream. Sex had been even more elusive than sleep in her life. Only difference was her current dry spell had lasted far longer than two weeks. Try two years, and then some.

"Get up. We have to leave." Even in telepathy, the words were too loud for comfort.

Renee struggled to a sit, the bedclothes tangling around her limbs. "It's the middle of the freaking night. Where are we going?"

"Why aren't you on your feet?" the bird demanded.

"Because I'm tired." She resisted the temptation to spell out t-i-r-e-d. Eagles didn't deal in subtlety. No raptor did, and her bondmate was one of the older animals and set in its ways. "Where are we going?" she repeated and tugged her legs out from beneath the sheets and blanket.

"South. We're shifting. We'll make better time in the air."

She shivered. It was cold in her bedroom. Grabbing a sweater, she wrapped it around herself. "Slow down. If we shift, I'll be stuck in your form wherever it is that has you so spun out. I need information before I fly out of here with nothing but feathers at my disposal."

Magic jabbed her just beneath her breastbone, prickly and insistent. "Stop it." Renee marshaled power of her own. "You can probably force a shift, but why would you want to piss me off? Talk with me, instead."

"For once, just do what I say. When have I ever led you astray?" The bird had switched tactics. Compulsion ran beneath its words, slick and sticky as sweet syrup.

"You don't really want me to answer that." She made her words just as saccharine. Her bondmate saw itself as invincible, but its tendency to forge ahead without thinking things through had created more than a few problems. Ticking them off on her fingers would only put the bird on the defensive.

After a flurry of beak clacks and annoyed bird noises, the eagle said, *"We must travel many leagues to the south. One of the oldest of us has bonded, and I would confer with it."*

Renee switched to telepathy, hoping to encourage more information. *"How many leagues, and will we be staying wherever this is?"*

"Many leagues, and of course we'll remain. Why wouldn't we?"

An image swam across Renee's visual field. She peered intently at it, recognizing Colorado's Rocky Mountains. Colorado was a big place, and it was hundreds of miles from her current location in Glasgow, Montana.

"What about my job?" she countered. *"I can't take off in the middle of the night without telling anyone."*

"Why not?"

Breath hissed through her teeth. *"Because we live in a human world. They all think I'm like them. It's how we survive. And it's not just my job. What about my home? All my things?"*

"You wouldn't be gone forever." No longer trying to convince her with magic, the eagle was being reasonable.

Renee floated some reason of her own. "If you want us to remain in Colorado for any amount of time, I'll need clothes. I'll need my car and all the accoutrements of my human form. If we go—and it's still an if in my book—I have to do this right."

"Right is shifting and flying out the door."

"No. Right is calling the hospital, giving them some excuse why I need time off, and paying an extra month's rent so the landlord doesn't lease this house out from under me."

"All that will take too long."

"But you said this elder animal had bonded. That means it's not going anywhere for at least the shifter's lifespan."

More clacking and squawking joined the wheezy sound the eagle made when it was pissed. Renee flicked on a bedside lamp and got up. No more sleep for her tonight, no matter what else transpired. She grabbed her tablet and began jotting down a to-do list. If she really was leaving for a while—and it appeared she was—she didn't want to forget anything.

The tablet's clock said it was four in the morning. Too early to ring up hospital administration and tell them she had a family emergency on the East Coast—

or better yet in Europe. She'd lived through several human lifespans. Every time she resurfaced, she crafted a slightly different story. Modern life with its emphasis on identifiers like social security numbers and DNA had made things harder to finesse, but not impossible.

The bird had fallen silent. She took it as a good sign. Compromise was the hallmark of all long-standing partnerships. By the time dawn was breaking, she'd tossed clothes into a duffel bag, showered, washed and dried her long, wheat-colored hair, and made some electronic deposits, including one to her landlord.

After a few calculations, she paid her utilities ahead and carted the duffel into the garage where she chucked it into the boot of her SUV. She hadn't been in northeast Montana long, only a little over a year. Her current life story, which she'd held onto through nursing school and the advanced degree that allowed her independent practice status as a family nurse practitioner, was a variation on her usual theme.

No immediate family. No ex-husbands. No children. The occasional well-meaning soul would suggest she get a pet, perhaps a nice, well-behaved dog or a cat. She always demurred. Too busy. She wasn't home enough to do much more than clean up and return to work.

The poor neglected canine would develop serious

issues, but they'd be nothing compared with its major meltdown once it sensed her dual nature.

She glanced at her tablet, checking off items on the list she'd thrown together. It was seven. Time to call the hospital. They wouldn't be pleased because they didn't have anyone who could replace her. She was a cheap alternative to an MD. Not that Valley General had come out and couched it in those terms, but they knew it, and so did she.

She dialed the number for hospital administration and stumbled through a half-assed excuse.

The personnel clerk just coming on shift hesitated before saying, "Sorry to hear about your aunt. Not that it's exactly my business, but I didn't realize you had any close family members."

"Not along the lines of a husband or parents or kids," Renee replied, "but Aunt Denise raised me after my folks were killed in a car crash when I was fifteen. She's not doing very well, and I'd have a hard time living with myself if she died without me seeing her one last time."

"Sure. Of course. I understand." The sound of clicking keys followed. "You have two weeks and a day of accumulated paid time off."

"Should be plenty. I'll be in touch." Renee rang off, not wanting to deal with any more awkward questions. Like where exactly in Munich her aunt lived, which airport she'd be flying out of, or if she needed any assistance taking care of her house while she was gone.

She peered into the fridge and dropped a block of cheese and a package of salami into a plastic shopping bag. Everything else went into the dumpster in front of her house. As ready as she could be, she collected her tablet, her laptop, and her phone. Once she'd checked all the doors and windows, locking everything, she took a last look around before hurrying into the garage and sliding behind the wheel.

She loved dawn but loving the promise of a fresh new day wouldn't keep her awake. She felt the eagle's restless presence within her, but it had won and probably wouldn't exert any further pressure.

Not until they got closer to their destination. She nosed the car out of the garage, hit the clicker to close the automatic door, and said, "I'll just stop for coffee and breakfast, and then we'll kill off some miles."

"I still think we should have flown," her bondmate mumbled.

"We can fly all you want, once we're there." She tried for a conciliatory tone, but the bird didn't reply.

After hitting the drive-through at Grind Away, her favorite coffee shop, she queried her Nav program and selected a route. It was over 800 miles, not likely she'd arrive today, but certainly by the middle of tomorrow. It would be soon enough. She'd caught wind of disturbing news and didn't want to drive so long she couldn't maintain a vigilant attitude. Vampires were on the prowl. If the rumors were to be believed, rogue mages had allied themselves with vamps, and the combination was a threat to shifters everywhere.

Not that there was even one other shifter in her quadrant of Montana. None she knew about, anyway. Long before the vampire issue surfaced, her kind had adopted—and stuck with—a very low profile. She remembered how things had deteriorated in the Old Country and why they'd left.

Long ago, magic was revered, and those like her objects of respect and devotion. Enter a few priests with fire in their eyes spouting drivel about how magical creatures were devil spawn, and it hadn't taken very many years—less than a single generation—for everything to change.

She'd escaped burning by the narrowest of margins and stowed away on a frigate not long afterward. Magic hid her presence from the bunch of rowdy men, and she'd helped herself liberally to both food and grog, amused by their speculations about who was taking more than their fair share. When the freighter docked in New York, she'd strolled out on deck and down the gangway, delighted at the shocked expressions on the men's faces.

When the captain's outraged shouts about paying

for her passage with a pound of pussy escalated into him chasing her, she switched from a saunter to a full-out gallop and concealed herself along the crowded quay. That had been 273 years ago. In all that time, she'd heard so little about vampires, she'd let herself hope they'd remained east of the Atlantic.

Maybe the vamp rumors were why her eagle was so insistent about finding the elder animal who was newly bonded with someone. The bond animals talked among themselves. They'd be furious about the vampire threat. In true animal form, they'd want to act, not sit around chewing the fat. She'd ask the eagle pointblank, but not until they were closer to their destination. Last thing she wanted to do was remind her partner of its earlier exhortations that they had to hurry.

Farmland and prairies flashed past her windshield, and she settled into the mindless place that was part of long road trips. She'd need a spot to land once she got to Colorado, and her old friends Stephan and Marie Lurie would be perfect. She and Marie had exchanged the occasional email, and it would be good to see her again. The more she thought about it, the better she liked her plan. She could leave her things with them, take her eagle form, and let her bondmate dictate their next moves.

After choking down a burger and fries, she spent

the night at The Duck Inn, a down-at-the-heels motel in southeast Wyoming. She wasn't hungry, but she needed fuel and hadn't wanted to take the time for a sit-down meal. The bed was hard and lumpy, and the room seedy enough, she warded it to be on the safe side.

She was more than a match for anything human, but she didn't want to have to explain away bloody remains if some thugs saw her as easy pickings. Phone calls and police reports would slow her down—and blow her story about catching a flight for Berlin right out of the water, if anyone in Glasgow happened to tune in to the news.

She should be heading west for the airport in Billings. Her current location in Wyoming was definitely off route. Human intelligence had limitations, but even the dumbest human could figure that out.

After a restless night, she was back on the road at dawn, having stopped for a large coffee, breakfast sandwich, and assorted pastries from a convenient Starbucks. She'd wanted a shower, but the one in her room had black mold growing in every crevice, and it stank to her sensitive nose.

No matter. She could clean up once she reached Stephan and Marie's. A glance at her gas gauge propelled her into one of the big chain truck stops. At least the weather had been cooperative. This time of year, it could go either way, and she was relieved she hadn't battled snow, wind, sleet, or hail. Not that it couldn't happen between here and Denver, but the uncomfortable pit of her stomach tingling when bad weather was imminent wasn't there.

She crossed into Colorado before she used telepathy to raise Marie. Her visit would be a surprise, and she wanted to give her old friend at least a small window of warning. After three tries, she switched to Stephan.

"Renee? That you?" His characteristic gruffness hadn't changed a bit, but she could have hugged him. When Marie hadn't answered, she'd started to worry they'd been casualties of the vampire incursion.

"Yes. Sorry for no notice, but I'll be there in a couple hours. I've been trying to reach Marie, but she's not answering."

"No. She wouldn't."

An odd undercurrent made her blood run cold. Before she could find a diplomatic way to ask why, Stephan went on. *"Hell of a way for you to find out, but Marie is dead."*

Tears stung the corners of Renee's eyes before they overflowed. She tried to get a handle on her emotions, but great, choking sobs pushed past her resolve. She pulled to the side of the interstate. Crying and driving didn't mix well. And guilt was a brassy bitch when it teamed up with twenty-twenty hindsight She should have made more of an effort to remain connected with her friend, but something always got in the way.

When she could do something other than cry, she asked, *"What happened?"*

"Not a tale for telepathy. We'll talk once you're here. Two hours, you say?"

"About that. Maybe three if I run into traffic."

"Be careful. Remain alert. Ward yourself. I assume you're alone."

"Yes, I am, but how'd you know?"

"How else?" he replied. *"You always are. Not that it's a curse or anything. I'm alone now too, and I don't see that changing. Don't want it to. Marie was the love of my life. The only woman for me."*

His words were simply spoken, heartfelt, resolute. They brought on a fresh spate of tears.

"Do you need me to meet you?" Stephan's question was laced with concern.

"Nah. I'm almost there. See you soon. And I'm so very sorry for your loss."

"She was your friend too." His words were soft before he broke their connection.

"Yeah," she spoke to the empty car. "That's the problem. I could have been a better friend."

All the rationalizations about shifters deciding it

was safest to live apart from one another didn't ease her guilt. She should have visited Marie, spent more time with her.

"Marie could have visited us too." The bird's comment came out of left field.

"Thanks." Renee swiped the back of one hand beneath her nose and funneled the car back into light traffic. She constructed a ward, determined not to fall prey to whatever had killed Marie. Stephan wouldn't have warned her if it wasn't necessary.

She followed up on her earlier hunch and asked, "What do you know about the vampire problem?"

"I already told you about a few disgruntled mages joining forces with them." A rough beak clack was followed by, *"They've always resented us."*

"I heard that part, about vamps mixing their magic with mage power. And I remember all about how much mages hated us. I was there when they escalated their ire to outright war. It's been hundreds of years since we migrated from the Old Country, though. In all that time, mages haven't been a problem. What changed?"

"I don't know the answer to that."

Something about the bird's bitten off reply suggested it knew more than it was letting on.

Renee picked her words with care. "Okay. You don't know for certain, but you're very wise and very old"—she laid it on thick—"and I bet you have a few working theories."

"What do you remember about solar and lunar cycles linked to astrology?"

The question caught her off-guard, and she culled through her memory banks. Where once she'd barely left her house without consulting either the daily juxtaposition of the planets or a tarot spread, she'd grown lax.

Yeah. Chalk it up to my years pretending to be human.

"We're coming to the end of a major cycle, aren't we? Like a 900-year one."

"Aye, that we are." The eagle reverted to Gaelic. *"But not 900 years. You're confusing an astrological age with something else. There are twelve astrological ages, one for each zodiac sign, and it takes roughly 26,000 years to complete a single cycle of twelve ages..."*

As she listened, knowledge returned in bits and pieces. "The transitions between ages always cause psychic unrest," she mumbled. "Which cycle is about to end, and which sign is up next?"

"Not so simple." The bird's tone was somber. *"We are coming to the close of an entire age. Pisces is on its way out after a rocky 2000-year tenure. Aries is up next, which isn't promising."*

She started to ask why not but bit back the words.

It was simple enough to figure out. Aries was ruled by Mars, god of war. It was a fire sign, hence volatile as fuck.

"What can we do about it?" She closed her teeth over her lower lip, biting hard to still a case of runaway nerves.

The bird hesitated so long, she was afraid it wasn't going to answer. Finally, it said, *"The other animals and I believe metaphysical backwash is responsible for the mages suddenly deciding now was the time to lash out. Vampires have always been bastards. They live for mayhem and sowing the seeds of chaos."*

Her navigation bot, a Brit with a to-die-for voice told her to take the next exit.

"That clarifies the why part—" she began.

"I know nothing for certain," the eagle broke in.

"All right, so maybe it clarifies why. Can we do something about it, or are the psychic forces at play too powerful for us to fight against?"

"That remains to be seen, but it's why I must join forces with the lion."

"That's who is newly bonded? You never did say which type of animal."

"Yes, but not just any lion." Pride threaded beneath the bird's words. *"This is the first lion shifter. It's a cave lion, and one of the wisest of us all. It has sought a*

bondmate for eons, but your numbers have dwindled until shifters are in danger of dying out entirely."

She murmured sympathetically. She didn't agree with the eagle about shifters hovering on the brink of extinction, but it had a tendency to overdramatize things. A far more likely explanation for the cave lion remaining mateless was it had been waiting for just the right shifter, one with extraordinary power, to bond with.

Two more turns, and she pulled onto the long drive leading to Stephan and Marie's ranch. It would always be Stephan and Marie's to her, and she hoped for ashes where she could pay her respects.

By the time she reached the sprawling farmhouse and parked off to one side of the yard, people had piled out of the house. She recognized Stephan and his niece, Sarai. The dark-haired, brown-eyed shifter with Sarai looked vaguely familiar, but she couldn't place him right off the bat.

Stephan yanked her car door open and scooped her onto her feet and into a hug. "It's good to see you, Renee." He was such a big man, he made her feel small crushed against him. His hair was still ice blond and his blue eyes crinkled at the corners.

The tears she'd thought she was past flooded her eyes again, and she hugged him back. "I'm so sorry. I wish—"

"Hush. I know. We all miss her."

Sarai's red hair fell in a single queue down her back. She pried Renee out of Stephan's arms and embraced her too. "I want you to meet my brand-new mate."

"Mate, is it?" Renee glanced at the dark-haired hunk with greater interest. "I know you, don't I?"

"Aye, lassie. That you do."

Renee laughed. "Even if I forgot you, Niall, which is unlikely, I'd never forget that sexy Irish brogue. Congratulations to the two of you."

"Thanks." Sarai smiled warmly, her blue eyes aglow with love.

A clatter from the front porch was followed by, "Morning, all. I really should get moving. No reason to take advantage of your hospitality."

Renee disentangled herself from Sarai and fell headlong into acres of broad-shouldered, long-legged man. Blond hair was cropped close to his head and keen blue eyes perched above defined cheekbones. A high forehead and squared-off chin added to his allure. Faded jeans rode low on his hips, and a worn chambray shirt was only buttoned partway.

He was quite possibly the most striking man she'd ever seen. She realized she was staring but couldn't help herself. Before she had a chance to correct the bad impression she must be making as a tongue-tied fool, her eagle shrieked, *"It's the lion. The lion."*

Amid the protest of ripping fabric as her clothing turned to shreds, the bird forced its way through, flying around everyone's heads in a broad swathe and cawing like a mad thing.

Great. Fucking great. Whoever Mr. Handsome is must think I'm a green, newly-minted shifter who can't control her magic.

Yeah, and any chance of him being interested in me as something beyond an object of derision and pity just flew right out the window.

The analogy of flying out windows and her eagle form struck a black humor note. If the bird wasn't using her vocal cords, she'd have laughed.

"It appears your bondmate is acquainted with Jeremiah's." Stephan grinned broadly. "Bond animals, I swear."

"Can't live with 'em, can't live without 'em," Sarai agreed, adding, "Sprinkle some of that Aquarius charm around, Renee. Might calm your eagle down."

Renee didn't bother to point out that a bond animal who was spun out enough to force a shift wouldn't be amenable to much of anything. The next circle around the group of shifters was tighter, and she wondered what the eagle was up to. Before she could issue a sharp suggestion to get itself under control, it divebombed the blond god, did a flip midair, and ended up perched on his shoulder, talons digging deep.

She'd thought her embarrassment couldn't get any worse.

She was wrong.

CHAPTER 3

Day Earlier

Jeremiah ended up helping Niall with the last of his moving after all. He'd slept for almost twelve hours after getting home. Luck had been with him. The other mages were still asleep when he'd shown up, so he'd been spared telling them about the miracle of his bondmate. Likewise, when he'd finally woken midday, the nine mages he shared a rambling Victorian with were either at work or off running errands.

If anyone had been home, he'd have told them about the lion. The information would have burst from him, impossible to keep under wraps. Perhaps the goddess was watching out for him, offering a small island of solitude until he got a better handle on his unexpected magical boon.

He grabbed a fast shower and a snack and left, planning to swing by Stephan's farm. His bondmate had imparted important information the previous night, perceptions he wanted to bounce off shifters who had some miles under their belts.

He'd been painfully honest when he told the cave lion he needed a crash course in being a shifter. Nothing titrated. Nothing held back. The lion had chuckled and suggested the following day would be soon enough for such a gargantuan endeavor.

His phone trilled when he was nearly to the interstate. He considered ignoring it until he checked the caller ID and saw Niall's name. The jaguar shifter restated his earlier offer, and it sounded better after a decent night's sleep. Jeremiah had turned the car toward Glenwood Springs and traded muscles for knowledge over the hours they crammed everything Niall couldn't part with into the farm truck. Once the items was loaded, Sarai talked him into coming home with them.

As soon as he agreed, she offered to drive with him. Jeremiah figured it was the lure of the Corvette, but she had a different ulterior motive. They hadn't been underway ten minutes before she pried his birth information out of him and used her phone to access an astrological program. By the time they got to her uncle's farm, she told him she'd sent his chart and solar return to his phone.

"Thanks. I'll need you to interpret all those runic symbols, though. I knew them once, and quite well, but I've grown rusty."

Sarai turned a million-watt smile his way. "No worries. These modern computer programs come with at least a lay explanation of all the major points. If you want anything in greater depth, ask away." Her grin widened. "I knew you had to be a Leo sun sign, with a whole lot of Leo scattered through your chart. Sag rising and a Scorpio moon make you a force to be reckoned with."

He chuckled. "Chloe always said I was hardheaded. Must mean kind of the same thing." He got out and went around to open her door.

"Come on in," Stephan called from the porch. "Dinner's ready. You can unpack later. Or tomorrow."

"I like the sound of that." Niall slid down from the truck's high cab. "Thanks for letting us use your pickup. Made this easier."

"Anytime." Stephan crooked two fingers. "Wash up and let's eat."

Jeremiah figured dinner had been ready for hours since it was pushing nine at night. He tucked into a savory lamb and vegetable stew, delighted to have a home-cooked meal.

Stephan waited until he was done eating before saying, "Niall and Sarai told me about the lion. How's it going?"

The question may have sounded rhetorical, but it deserved a thoughtful answer. "My new magic will take a whole lot of getting used to. I don't want to bring shame to my new bondmate—or myself."

"The lion wouldn't have picked you if it expected you to fall short," Stephan said gruffly.

Rather than addressing his considerable set of concerns about his new magic, Jeremiah said, "Last night, I asked it about the vampire problem."

Niall furled both dark brows. "Aye? And what did it have to say?"

"Several things. I was actually on my way here when you nabbed me earlier today and pitched your case about needing my back rather than my brains."

Stephan tipped the flagon of red wine into Jeremiah's mug and murmured, "Sounds like thirsty business."

"Thanks." Jeremiah drank deep and focused his next words on Sarai. "Part of this will be right up your alley. Apparently, we're near the end of a full cycle of astrological ages. When one age merges into the next, there're always supernatural shock waves, but it's heightened by a factor of ten at the close of a complete cycle."

Sarai drew her mouth into a thoughtful expression, lips pressed together. "I'm sure your bondmate is correct about an astrological age drawing to a close. Problem is they last so long, it's rare for shifters to live through even a single transition, so it isn't something I've paid much attention to."

"Not just one age." Jeremiah wanted to make certain she grasped the cave lion's message. "If I understood correctly, this is the close of an entire cycle of twelve ages, which is what makes it so dangerous."

"Oh my. That would make quite a difference," she murmured.

"Anyway," Jeremiah continued, "we have a fairly narrow window, maybe as little as a year, to unravel the mages' alliance with vampires."

"What happens if we fail?" Niall asked, his usual cocky confidence notably absent.

"If we segue into the next age, one ruled by Aries, without fixing this mess, something about a surfeit of psychic emanations will spell our doom." He slogged down the rest of his wine before continuing, "I didn't fully understand how that last part would work, or why these supernatural wavelengths couldn't function in our favor, but the cave lion was most emphatic we had to take an aggressive stance."

Stephan eyed his niece. "Can you find out more about the zodiac link to all this?"

She nodded solemnly. "Tomorrow. I'll go to my shop and cull through my reference books. I have a lot of them. Surely, something this major will have gotten some pen-time."

Niall rose from the table. "Probably as good an opportunity as any to call it a night," he said, sounding subdued. Nothing like the Niall who'd faced off against Jeremiah and called him untrustworthy after his ploy to mow through a vampire horde had succeeded.

"Want to bunk here?" Stephan asked Jeremiah as he stood and began gathering dishes into his arms.

"Sure, but only if you let me take care of the dishes."

"It's a deal. I'll just carry them into the kitchen, and then they're all yours. Take the second-to-the-last room on the right."

Jeremiah lingered over the dishes, soothed by the ambiance in Stephan's home. The energy was different from being surrounded by mages, but that was understandable. What surprised him was how quickly he took to his new affiliation. He'd assumed there'd be more of a transition period. When he finally lay down in a well-appointed room that looked as if it did double duty as an office, he slept like a dead thing.

He'd meant to be up early and on his way, but he overslept. A commotion out in the yard ended up driving the final vestiges of sleep away. Staggering upright, he peered out a window and saw the sun already high in the sky. A beat-up blue SUV was parked off to one side. The car hadn't been there the previous night, and he wondered who it belonged to.

He didn't have to wonder long.

A leggy blonde stood a few feet away with Stephan's arms around her. The woman's hair was platinum with golden streaks running through it. Clear, green eyes were widely set and tilted just enough to suggest a hint of Asian blood. Snug jeans vanished into well-worn leather boots, and a stretchy top offered a clear outline of generous breasts as she transitioned from Stephan's embrace to Sarai's.

He was staring, but the newcomer was exotic and gorgeous. He itched to make a grab for her high, tight ass. As if in full agreement, his cock rose in a column and pressed against his belly. He hadn't had sex in so long, he wasn't sure if the hiatus was measured in months or years.

He'd thought he'd moved beyond spontaneous physical reactions to female beauty, but his hard-on made a liar out of him.

Jeremiah moved away from the window, feeling like a lecherous peeping Tom. Maybe he could just pop out onto the porch and introduce himself. Find out who the knock-your-eyes-out blonde was, but he'd be subtle about it.

It wouldn't do to fall all over her. Hell, she might have a mate for all he knew. He decided on a generic greeting, one that would give him an easy out, and pushed his hard-on to a less obvious position, masking it with a glob of magic. He'd slept in his clothes, so all he had to do was slide his stockinged feet into his boots and lace them.

Being noisy on purpose, he walked through the house and out onto the porch, letting the door bang a bit. "Morning, all," he called cheerily, aiming a pleasant nod at the blonde woman. "I really should get moving. No reason to take advantage of your hospitality."

He kept his expectations low. Hell, he'd have been delighted if the woman introduced herself, but her actions knocked him off balance. Magic shimmered hotly around her, clothing shredded, and an enormous eagle took shape. Screeching like a mad thing, it flew around everyone's heads in uneven ellipses. Right before her shift, he thought he'd picked up on telepathy alluding to a lion, which might mean him.

"It appears your bondmate is acquainted with Jeremiah's." Stephan grinned broadly at the eagle flapping madly overhead. His words clinched Jeremiah's suspicion the lion was indeed him.

"Bond animals, I swear." Niall snickered.

"Can't live with 'em, can't live without 'em," Sarai agreed, adding, "Sprinkle some of that Aquarius charm around, Renee. Might calm your eagle down."

Renee. The blonde woman is named Renee.

Before he could react to the tableau unfolding around him, the bird made a dive for his shoulder and latched on, talons pinching through flesh. He resisted the temptation to smile and say something like, "Honey, you can latch onto me any old time."

This wasn't about him or sex. The eagle knew his lion. What that meant remained to be seen.

"We are shifting," the lion informed him. *"The eagle is a very old companion of mine. Would you prefer to salvage your clothing?"*

"Thank you for offering me a choice." Suddenly shy, he glanced at the house.

Stephan caught on fast—or maybe he'd been listening in—and trotted up the stairs and onto the porch. He held out an arm. "Land here," he told the eagle in a tone that didn't leave any space for disagreement "We will offer privacy for Jeremiah to shift. It's far from second nature for him."

With a disconsolate squawk, the bird spread its wings bnd coasted to Stephan's extended arm.

Jeremiah's shoulder hurt. Blood dripped from where the eagle's talons had cut through his flesh. He ignored it and hurried inside, shucking and folding clothing as soon as he was on the other side of the door. Naked, he opened himself to magic and reveled in the sense of wonder that accompanied altering his form. Now that he understood what the sensations meant, where they'd lead, he didn't fight the transformation.

The pain he remembered from his first shift in the cave never materialized, only a few minor discomforts as bone, muscle, and skin rearranged themselves. A phalanx of questions filled his mind, but a lot of them would be answered soon. No reason to bother his bondmate.

He padded toward the front door, enjoying the fluid grace in his animal body. The lion directed a small shot of power, and the latch released. Between paw and snout, it muscled the door wide enough to sashay through.

Stephan had moved back down the steps and stood in the yard, the eagle still perched on his forearm much as a hunting hawk would have. Niall and Sarai lounged nearby. Jeremiah tried to glom onto the sense of belonging that had filled him last night, but it was elusive.

Right now, balancing from paw to paw as he moved down the steps, he felt like an imposter. The fastest way to get over it was to face it, but he'd deal with his issues later. The bird launched itself off Stephan's arm and circled, landing with its feet on the lion's broad back. The beast took off at an easy lope, heading for a band of forested hills beyond Stephan's farm.

"*Who are you?*" rolled through his mind.

At first, he figured it was the eagle, but why would it care? The animals didn't have names, which meant it must be the woman.

"*Can you not hear me?*" the same voice asked. A pleasant contralto, it reminded him of heavy cream, rich and silky.

"*Sorry. I'm sorry,*" he replied. "*This is all so new to me. Not telepathy, but the shifter side of things. I'm Jeremiah Fuller. Up until a couple of days ago, I was a mage.*"

"*What? But that's not possible.*" The honeyed tone vanished, replaced by strident disbelief.

"*How do you think I feel about it?*" he tossed back, quickly adding, "*Not that I'm not humbly grateful, but still, it's a rather large change.*" Magic flared between lion and eagle, so he figured they were holding a conversation of their own.

"*Are you one of the mages that joined with vampires?*" Suspicion lined her words.

"*Oh hell no. It was only a few of the Mages First group who fell off the rails.*"

"*How many is a few?*" Her tone remained glacial. "*And who the hell are Mages First?*"

He recalled the enmity between their people, certain she did as well. *"Mages First is who's left from the ones still steeped in bitterness from our old war. Perhaps as many as a hundred remain, which is a fraction of their original number. We've captured them as we found them, separating them from their magic."*

"Why not kill them?"

"Could you murder a kinsman in cold blood?"

His answer seemed to sink in because she hesitated before saying, *"It wouldn't be easy."*

He considered telling her the whole story about the vampires and the poison, but it felt too convoluted. She might take the same tack Niall had and decide he'd been foolhardy and put shifters at unnecessary risk to carry out his secret agenda.

He had no idea why, but how she viewed him was important, and he didn't want to make things worse.

"How is it you're a shifter?" she asked after they'd been silent for a while.

The flash and flare of magic as he ran with the eagle clinging to his back suggested the bond animals were deep in talking or catching up or hatching plans. He supposed he could have figured out a way to listen in—maybe—but Renee had asked him a question.

Niall kept his answer simple. *"I was gravely ill, close to death. One of your healers saved my life. Only thing I could figure was I absorbed enough of his magic through the healing to turn the tides. According to my bondmate, our magic springs from common roots."*

"I know that. I'm one of the old ones."

He wanted to ask where she hailed from. If she had family. If she had a mate. But she didn't seem in the mood for small talk—or trading histories.

"Sorry," she added. *"That was surly, and there's no call. I have to trust you're walking the good side of the street. If you weren't, the cave lion would never have bonded with you."*

"How did your eagle know about me?" he asked, genuinely curious.

A rippling snort was followed by, *"It didn't know about you, only that your bond animal had forged a linkage. You're why I'm here. I was sound asleep in my bed in Glasgow, Montana when the eagle woke me and told me we had to find you as fast as we could."*

"It's the vampire thing, huh?"

"Yup. I'm not sure how much you know about being a shifter—"

"Very little," he broke in. *"Only what Niall and Sarai told me yesterday."*

"Some of this may be a repeat, but the animals all know one another. They inhabit a special world that's closed to everyone but them. All of them, bonded or not, can meet and converse in their world, but they cannot effect any changes here on earth unless they're bonded.

Something about the shifter bond enables their magic, moves it from philosophical possibility to reality."

He was considering the ramifications of that when she started talking again. *"From what my bird told me, the lion has long sought a worthy bondmate, which was why I assumed you'd be a very powerful magic-wielder."*

"I am, just not of the shifter variety." He stopped there. Her implication that shifters were the only ones with potent magic rankled.

The lion wheeled, changing directions and heading back toward Stephan's farm.

"Are you affiliated with other mages? Or do you work alone?"

Her question caught him off-guard. *"I live with several other mages."*

"Mmph. Bet they all want bond animals now too."

"They don't know about me. Not yet."

"Why not?" Her words held barbed edges.

"Not for the reasons you're thinking." He hated being backed into corners, and defensiveness ran through him in a thin, bitter tide.

"How would you know what I'm thinking?"

"I hear it in your tone. You assume I'm ashamed of my new magical status, but that's not it at all. I've been a shifter for a grand total of less than forty-eight hours.

For the brief period when I was home, either no one else was awake, or they weren't there."

He clammed up. He didn't owe her a thing. Not explanations. Not excuses. Nothing. So what if her bondmate and his were old chums?

He picked up the pace, and the lion didn't fight him. Once he started moving faster, the bird took off, winging skyward until he couldn't see it anymore. When they trotted into Stephan's front yard, he kept right on going up the steps. A judicious blast of magic opened the door, and he cruised through intent on shifting, dressing, and leaving.

The blonde might be a knockout, but she had too many prickly edges for his taste. She'd said she was one of the older shifters. It meant she'd lived through the long-running war between his kin and hers. Losses on both sides had been crippling. Just because he'd found a way to come to terms with it didn't mean she had.

He dressed quickly and was halfway out the door when Stephan, Niall, and Sarai trooped up the front steps.

"You're not leaving," Stephan said. "Not yet, anyway."

"We want to know what the animals came up with," Sarai chimed in.

"Aye. We went hunting for Renee but couldn't find

her," Niall said. "Her car's here, so we figure she's still flitting about in her bird form."

Jeremiah wasted all of five seconds feeling pleased Renee hadn't left. He shut it down fast—she certainly wasn't hanging around because of him—and nodded pleasantly at the trio staring at him. "I'm not sure what the animals discussed, but I'd be glad to ask the lion."

Stephan sent a strange look scudding his way but stopped short of chastising him for not giving the animals' conversation top priority when it was happening.

"You do that, son." Stephan dropped into one of the chairs scattered around the porch. "Take a load off and let us know what your bondmate has to say."

Jeremiah hooked a boot around the bottom of a chair and positioned it for sitting. He turned his attention inward. *"Everyone's waiting,"* he said. *"Tell us what happened."*

"I will share what you need to know. No more. No less."

Jeremiah opened his mind and heart, encouraging his bondmate to begin talking. He'd show the pesky, sanctimonious eagle shifter mage power wasn't to be trifled with. Or discounted. He was here. She wasn't. It gave him an edge, and he was shameless enough to grab the advantage and run with it.

CHAPTER 4

Renee had been listening to the eagle's conversation with half an ear, so she missed a whole lot of whatever it kicked around with the cave lion. When her bondmate had mentioned the words *cave lion*, she'd sketched out a mental image that didn't come close to doing the beast justice.

It was magnificent. Huge and regal with a golden mane that fell around its shoulders. Silvery flecks made its eyes luminous, and its paws were the size of platters and tipped with black claws four inches long. Riding on the creature's back felt like an honor—until the magic wielder attached to it revealed he'd been a mage until something like thirty-five seconds ago.

What the unholy fuck? A mage?

Mages held inferior magic. They were the po' folk cousins in her magical lineup, and she'd never had much truck with them. Her interest in the hunky blond man turned into suspicion, and she peppered him with questions.

Most of them verged on rude, insolent enough she'd forced herself to apologize at one point but hadn't been happy about it. The mage, or shifter, or whatever the hell he was, had become testy.

She didn't blame him, but it was beyond the point.

She still rode on the lion's back but was increasingly anxious to leave. Finally, she turned her full attention to the eagle, hoping to hasten their egress. At first, its part of the conversation felt disjointed, like it wasn't a match for the lion's comments.

"Touché," the bird squawked, sounding irritated.

"Not it at all," the lion countered. "You missed my point."

"No. You missed mine. You've lived in our other world too long. Your ideas may have worked a millennium ago, but not now."

"You can't know that."

"Aye. I can. Damn it. You're every bit as stubborn as you've always been."

"And you're not?" the lion asked in a patronizing tone.

Protectiveness for her eagle blasted through her. They weren't accomplishing anything here, so she made a grab for command of the bird's body, surprised when it didn't lodge a complaint as she spread its wings and pumped them, gaining altitude quickly.

Renee didn't mince words. *"I missed the first part of that. What did the lion want to do that you disagreed with?"*

"It thinks we should gather all the bond animals and storm the vampires' central location. Except there isn't one. Not anymore."

She hadn't been aware vamps even had anything like a headquarters. Hundreds of years ago, their powerbase was located in Transylvania, but that time was long past. Vampires hailed from central Romania, an area bordered to the east by the Carpathian Mountains. Others with magic had avoided it, even if it was inconvenient. Once the war with the mages heated up, she'd all but forgotten about vampires.

"Hmmm. All the bond animals, means the shifter half too. Right?"

"Unless you've come up with a clever way to separate us," the bird snarked back.

Marshaling forces in an all-out confrontation might not be such a bad idea. At least it would bring things to a head quickly. She started to dig deeper, but the eagle must have been monitoring her thoughts because it said, *"You're wrong too. Just like the lion."*

"Why?"

The eagle clacked its beak sharply together. *"It's*

not like it was before we crossed the sea. Vampires are not concentrated in a single location. If we use maximum force on one bastion, the other vampires will go to ground."

Renee understood the problem. Vampires weren't alive. They required blood to function at an optimal level, but they could enter a sort of stasis where they required nothing. Not blood or air. Certainly not food since they never ate anyway. If they were spooked, they could sequester themselves in spots where no one could find them.

Worse, if mages holed up with them, goddess only knew what horror would emerge. Her distrust of the mage who'd bonded with the cave lion roared to the forefront.

"I don't like any of this."

"Nor do I. It's why I didn't protest when you flew away." The eagle soared higher before diving to scoop up a hapless mouse, crunching tender bones with its sharp beak.

She considered winging her way back to Stephan's, turning the car around, and going home. She could smooth things over at work, spreading magic about as she layered new lies over the old ones. Her co-workers would believe her, no matter how fantastic her story, but how could she turn her back on her kinsmen? The vampire problem wouldn't go away. Neither would the asshole mages who'd thought it was funny or smart or some twisted form of divine justice to lend their power to darkness.

Her next question came hard. *"Did you sense the lion had been corrupted? Turned to evil?"*

"No, but I fail to understand why it joined its star with a mage. Not when it could have had its choice of any shifter."

Renee chose not to remind her bondmate of its earlier assertion that there were no shifter candidates to form new bonds with, because they were dying out. *"We need to go back to Stephan's house. I want to pay my respects to Marie if I can. Once we're there, we can figure out our next moves."* She paused for a beat. *"Are you finished talking with the lion?"*

"Probably not, but for now I am. It believes the animal portion of the shifter bond should be in charge of planning and executing our offensive. That approach won't work."

She'd gathered as much from the eagle's earlier comment about everyone shifting and launching a major offensive. It was exactly the type of thing they would have done a few hundred years before, but the exigencies of living in the twenty-first century meant shifters spent very little time in their animal forms. The cave lion probably wasn't aware of that.

Annoyance cut deep. The lion might be ancient

and powerful, but those two elements didn't excuse it from taking how things worked now into consideration. Shifters hadn't fought in any kind of organized fashion since the tail end of the mage war. No general worth his salt dragged rusty troops forward without honing them into an efficient unit.

Maybe the lion assumed the animals would follow its lead blindly, but those days were over too. The human half of the shifter partnership had controlled the relationship for so long, it was rare for a bondmate to insist on ascendency like her bird had done when it forced a shift in Stephan's yard.

She was deep in thought, flying mindlessly in the general direction of her car when a dizzying wave of magic rocked her. She snapped out of her reverie fast, scanning the tree canopy below.

"What the hell was that?" she asked and draped warding around them.

"I don't know."

Another blast of magic battered her. To her horror, they were losing altitude. Her wings were still flapping, but something was wrong with the air. It wasn't solid enough to give them purchase. She flapped harder, but it made no difference. The bird sank faster than before.

It feathered its wings and latched a talon around a passing evergreen bough, catching it handily and averting their plunge to the earth beneath them. Breath puffed through her beak in little panting gasps, and she tightened her talons around the branch to establish a better grip.

"We need to shift," the eagle said. *"If I can't fly, I'm helpless. We're better off in our other body."*

She reluctantly agreed, but the top of a fir tree was nowhere to finesse a shift. Heart pounding, she eyed a lower branch, let go of the first one, and dropped. Two more branch trades put her in reasonable position to shinny down the tree. If flying was off the plate, maybe her magic wouldn't shield her from a fall, either.

No matter. She could downclimb from her current perch. The unpleasant magic that had sucked lift out of the air seemed to have left. Even if it wasn't gone, it was leaving them alone. Once she was human, she'd see about casting a teleport spell.

More than one way to skin a cat.

If she had enough magic—and it didn't backfire— she'd use her home as a focal point and worry about collecting her car later. Plan B was returning to Stephan's.

One step at a time. First, she had to shift. Once she had arms and legs, she'd work her way out of the tree. Her magic was sluggish, slow to heed her call. Its laggardly response shot her anxiety into orbit. Getting stuck between forms was serious business and could easily mean her death.

She forgot about business as usual and pulled power as hard and fast as she could. When feathers ceded to skin and hair, she exhaled noisily. Goddess be damned. If it was this hard to shift, how the hell would she manage to teleport once she was on the ground? She stopped thinking. It was counterproductive. Bark scratched her skin, drawing blood as she shinnied down from her perch. She didn't trust launching travel spells from trees. Something about their energy wasn't a good match for teleporting. She'd gotten tangled up in a tree spanning several worlds once, and it had taken her days to find her way back to Earth.

It wasn't an experience she was eager to repeat.

She was bleeding from multiple abrasions when her bare feet connected with the rocky dirt beneath the tree. Out of habit, she thanked the fir for being steadfast. It paid to acknowledge the natural world.

An icy wind made goose bumps rise along her exposed flesh. Wishing for clothes, she started to divert magic to heal her scrapes, but it wasn't wise. She needed every fragment of power at her disposal, and she'd burned through bunches shifting. Wasting what remained would be foolhardy.

"Get us out of here," the bird screeched.

Renee knew better than to waste time asking why. After the bird's strident warning, she felt darkness bearing down on them too. The perfidious air that hadn't been thick enough to keep them airborne was suddenly so dense it made breathing difficult. Her skin prickled unpleasantly, and she shivered from more than the forty-degree ambient temperature.

She threw her magical well wide open and visualized Stephan's house. It was closest, and this would be nip and tuck—if it worked at all. The air shimmered, glistened, and then blew back at her like an errant rubber band, slapping her hard across her entire body.

She yelped but made a grab for her spell, determined to make it work.

Maniacal laughter battered her from all sides, growing ever louder. She tried once more to escape, but this attempt was weaker than her first had been. At least the backlash wasn't as severe.

Footsteps pounded toward her. She might not be able to teleport out of here, but she could fight. Renee redirected her failing power and spun in a circle, determined to mete out as much damage as possible before the fuckers who had her in their gunsights killed her.

A noxious stench joined the unnaturally dense air. Rotten, dead smells that burned her nostrils and twisted her stomach into a harsh knot.

Vampires.

Nothing else smelled quite so putrid. She

swallowed back bile. She could puke later—if there was a later. Her thoughts flitted to Marie. Was this what happened to her? Poor, gentle Marie was anything but a warrior.

Two vamps trotted into view and then two more approached from the other direction. Light on their feet, they were garbed in modern clothing. No robes for this crew. All had luxuriant dark hair and the ungodly beauty characteristic of their race. They might be fuckers, but they were beautiful fuckers with chiseled planes in their faces. High smooth foreheads, squared-off jaws, arched cheekbones, and the barest hint of dark stubble.

Being Hollywood gorgeous made it easy for them to lure and immobilize prey. She was staring, as caught up in their hypnotic draw as the greenest human would have been.

She ground her teeth. She knew better, goddammit. Ripping her gaze from hot masculine perfection that oozed sex appeal—if you didn't have to smell them—she raised her hands and let power flow from her outstretched fingertips. Small flames jumped the gap between her and the vamps but fizzled before reaching them.

She tried harder. Directed more power, but with the same lack of results.

One of the vamps stepped forward, focusing liquid,

dark eyes on her. "You can keep it up until you drain your magic, which would be fine except we don't have time to wait for you."

"Or you can come with us straight away," another vamp, this one with silvery eyes, cut in. "If you don't turn this into a pitched battle, things will go easier for you."

"Come with you? I don't think so." Renee stood tall, excruciatingly aware of her nakedness. Beyond glomming onto handy veins, vampires' second favorite pastime was fucking.

The first vamp shrugged and made come-along motions with one hand. "Fine. Keep on lobbing power. We'll humor you for a while."

"*We can do this,*" the eagle said. "*I'll help.*"

Five more volleys convinced her she didn't possess enough power to break through whatever was warding the vampires. Not that she could have done much more than make their lives mildly uncomfortable, but her efforts were truly meaningless, even with her bondmate's help.

"*Keep going,*" the bird exhorted, punctuating its words with a screech.

"*No point. We'll fritter through all our magic for nothing.*"

The vampire with dark eyes furled his brows. "Are we done?"

"For now." She tried not to be obvious about panting, but she was scared and out of options. Swathing herself with phony aplomb, she turned abruptly and walked away from the four vampires wondering why they didn't come after her.

Her answer materialized in twenty feet when she ran into an invisible barrier that packed an electrical wallop so strong she landed on her ass. Scrambling upright and dusting dirt off her butt, she switched to her psychic view. A blackened perimeter had fused to the network of ley lines. The casting had mage stamped all over it, and she cursed the goddess-blasted one who'd bonded with the lion—and all his kin.

Highhanded fuckers.

Doing her damnedest to hang onto a few scraps of dignity, she turned slowly and crossed her arms beneath her breasts. "It's a sin against the goddess to pervert the ley lines. Their energy is the glue that holds Earth together. What do you want with me?"

"Pfft. We never cared about your stupid lines. Or your insipid rules. Phase one of our experiment is complete," the silver-eyed vampire said.

"I don't understand what that means," she retorted. "Or what it has to do with me." She scanned the sky, furious Gaia hadn't burst from the heavens to punish the vampire for sacrilege.

Except things never worked that way. She'd never

met any of the gods or goddesses. For all she knew, they were the purview of myth and not real at all.

"It means we understand how to augment our power from the mage side of your magical line. We're moving up. Many of us desire an animal form to morph into."

A raucous shriek from her bird nearly deafened her.

Another vampire, this one with sky-blue eyes, grinned, displaying very white teeth—and fangs. "I heard that. Birds are natural companions for us."

She swallowed hard, a tough job since her throat was dry as a dust-choked plain. "Why might that be?"

"The strongest of us have always been capable of flight." The creature leered at her.

Renee's stomach lurched sourly. She'd heard rumors about vampires flying, but never believed them. One thing was certain. She'd kill herself before she allowed these brazen bastards to turn her into an Auschwitz experiment. Maybe she could get them talking. If she could divert their attention, perhaps she could blast her way out of this mess.

She'd only get one chance, though.

"That's really interesting, about you flying," she murmured.

"We thought it would appeal to you," blue-eyes said.

You have no idea.

"It does," she purred. "I sense mage power clinging to you, yet there are no mages here. How did you manage that?"

The one with dark eyes sidled close. "Fools. They opened their magical centers to us. Once we were linked, we wedged the channel open." A harsh laugh blasted from between his chiseled lips and he shrugged. "They're ours now. And so is their power."

She held onto a bland expression with everything in her. What she wanted was to howl her outrage to the skies. She might distrust mages, but they'd been duped, mesmerized by vampire mind control. Poor stupid fools. It served them right, but even they deserved a chance to make a better choice.

"*Steady.*" The bird breathed the word into her mind.

She sucked air into uncooperative lungs. Her bondmate was right. She could save her bottomless fall into horror and outrage for after she was safe.

If that ever happened. Escape felt remote, but she couldn't give up.

"I had no idea you were so strong." She delivered as close an approximation to a fetching smile as she could manage. The vamps were so egotistical, they'd probably buy it.

"She appreciates us." Silver eyes strode to her side and wrapped an arm around her.

His touch gave her the creeps. She had to move fast, or her antipathy would bleed through and her seat-of-the-pants plan would never work. She glanced from one vampire to the next. "You were just teasing about being able to fly. Right?"

The dark-eyed one walked close enough to thump an index finger against her naked breastbone. "We never joke. It's not a vampire trait."

"Well then"—she held her ground and hoped her unsteady voice wouldn't give her away—"come fly with me. I love company in the air, and very few shifters are birds."

Without waiting for them to answer, she summoned shift magic, gratified it was more responsive than it had been transitioning from bird to human. Before her wings were fully feathered, she launched herself into the air— air that mercifully held her this time—and cawed merrily.

Would they fall for her challenge? If they did, it would divert enough of their magic, she could make good on her escape.

She hoped.

In her experience, arrogant bullies couldn't resist a contest to prove their talents. She engaged in an aerial ballet, dipping, diving, banking, even doing forward and backward flips to entice them to join her. They'd said some vampires could fly. What if none of these four were included in *some?*

After a heart-stopping pause where nothing happened—but at least they didn't snare her in magic to force her back to earth—she felt the same harsh jolt of power that had driven her to abandon her eagle form. Except this time, it wasn't aimed at her.

She flew another circle eight, keeping an eye on two of the vampires who'd leapt skyward. Rather like ungainly bats, their flight lacked elegance, precision. They might be airborne, but it looked neither natural nor comfortable. No wonder they wanted a bird to bond with.

The thought galvanized her into action. The eagle had been ready for her next move, though, and added its considerable ability to the mix. She'd no sooner visualized Stephan's farmhouse than the transport magic swept her into its maw. She slammed the magical back door hard to ensure the vamps couldn't follow her trajectory and forced herself to keep breathing.

The darkness characteristic of teleport spells ceded to light almost immediately. She scanned what was forming around her with anxious eyes. Had she succeeded? Or had the vamps subverted her spell and drawn her right back into their midst?

She shifted before her feet touched down and grappled for the small dirk she always wore attached to a thigh sheath. A magical accoutrement, it survived shifts, vanishing when she was a bird and reappearing when she was human. It wouldn't kill a vampire, but she could plunge it into her own breast.

Blinking hard, knife at the ready, she willed the mist around her to part.

"Renee!" Sarai's shout was the most welcome sound she'd ever heard.

Arms closed around her, and she fell into the wolf shifter's arms, not quite believing she was safe.

"*Safe for the moment,*" the eagle corrected her. "*Nowhere is safe anymore.*"

CHAPTER 5

Jeremiah was behind the wheel of his Corvette and partway down the long driveway when magical turbulence caught his attention. Stephan, Niall, and Sarai had chastised his bondmate nine ways from Sunday once he'd shared its ideas. Listening to them, he had to admit they'd floated some solid points.

Aside from a few heated snarls, the lion had remained silent throughout the discussion.

Still figuring things out, feeling his way as a newly-minted shifter, Jeremiah was headed back to Silverthorne to include his kin in a strategy session about how they approached the mage-fueled vampire dilemma. Renee hadn't returned, and the others were worried about her protracted absence.

He was too, but not enough to stick around for a

second session with the sharp side of her tongue. He braked hard and spun the Vette around in case the others needed him. He was close enough, he had to check out the volley of power. It had been too potent to be accidental.

He peeled into the yard to see a very naked Renee clasped in Sarai's arms. Stephan patted her heaving shoulders, and he realized she was sobbing. What in the goddess's name had happened?

Exiting the Vette, he stopped dead, uncertain what to do beyond staring at Renee. Her body was exquisite, perfect. Shapely shoulders led to a delicately curved spine and the kind of ass he'd assumed had to be hiding beneath her tight jeans. The flare of hips and the globes of her ass stole his breath. His erection from earlier roared back, pressing uncomfortably against the front of his pants.

Niall crossed the yard to where he stood. "Good you came back. Sure and 'tisn't safe for any of us to be alone. Stephan told Renee that, but she didn't listen."

"What happened to her?"

"Don't know yet," Niall replied. "She blasted into the yard, shifted, and when Sarai hugged her, she started sobbing." He frowned. "I've known Renee for a long time. She's not the crying type and doesn't rattle easily, so I figure whatever it is has to be pretty bad."

Grateful for something to think about other than

his unruly appendage, Jeremiah said, "Should we get her inside?"

"Sarai and Stephan are on it." Niall gestured toward them herding Renee into the house.

Jeremiah started after them, but Niall clamped a hand around his upper arm. "Let's give them a moment or two. Long enough for Renee to get her clothes on and for you to jog a few laps around the yard."

"That obvious, huh?" Jeremiah rearranged himself, but the front of his pants still looked as if someone had stuffed socks down them.

Niall snorted. "I don't have to look. Shifters have very sensitive noses, and desire holds a unique tang." He tugged on Jeremiah's arm. "Walk with me. She was with you. What happened?"

"What didn't?" He fell into step next to the jaguar shifter. "Once she found out I was as mage, she turned hostile. Peppered me with questions. Didn't trust my answers. I'm afraid I grew a bit testy after she suggested mages should murder the miscreants who signed on to be vampire minions."

"And then?" Niall pressed.

"She flew off. I was surprised when I returned and she wasn't here, but not that surprised. She was angry. I'm guessing she has a temper and was venting it in flight."

Niall creased his forehead in thought. "She may

have been irritated, but she's not one to hang onto a grudge. Of course, 'tis been a couple hundred years since I last spent much time with her, but she was one of the more even-tempered of us."

"You knew her from the Old Country?"

"Aye, that I did. She's always been a healer. Has the knack to coax chakras into alignment, and the sense to ease the dying to the other side when keeping them alive is an exercise in futility."

"Is she a doctor?"

Niall angled his head to one side. "I don't know. Not for certain. But I bet she earns her way at something close to it."

"So do you," Jeremiah pointed out. "Mr. Paramedic."

"Sure and 'tis true enough, but she has a genuine calling. Me, I just enjoy a fast-paced job that's never the same two days running. I'm not bad at assessing what's amiss, but I'm less good at mending what's broken."

Jeremiah angled a pointed look downward. "I'm fit for civilized company now. Let's go inside. I want to hear what happened, and I'd rather not hear it secondhand."

"Good enough." Niall clapped him on the back.

Jeremiah hesitated, but words forced themselves out before he could stop them. "Is Renee mated?"

"She wasn't when we left the British Isles, but that could have changed."

"What kind of man would send her here alone?" Fierce protectiveness raced through him, as much of a surprise as his question had been.

"Hard to say, mate. A man with a job, perhaps? One he couldn't leave easily. Shifter women have an independent streak, though. Even if she has a mate, they wouldn't necessarily be glued together at the hip."

Jeremiah grinned crookedly. "I know what you mean. Our females are hell on wheels. I'm surprised we haven't died out from them cutting our balls off."

Niall laughed. "Och, women. Yet I wouldn't wish to live without them."

"Nor would I."

They reached the front steps, and Jeremiah bounded up them. After knocking once, he strode through the door with Niall right behind him. Stephan, Sarai, and Renee sat at the kitchen table with a bottle of something that looked alcoholic between them.

"There you are," Stephan glanced their way. "Pull up a chair. I told Renee to hang onto her tale until we were all inside."

Niall slid in next to his mate and wrapped an arm around her. Sarai turned and kissed his cheek.

Jeremiah shifted from foot to foot; his bold words about not wanting secondhand news festered. That might be what he desired, but not if it caused Renee pain. He'd done enough damage for one day since she'd flown into danger to get away from him.

He clasped his hands behind him and directed his words at her. "I would like to hear your story, but not if my presence unnerves or offends you." He bowed his head slightly. "You were angry with me. It's why you left—and the reason for whatever happened to you. For that, I am truly sorry."

"For Christ's sake, sit down," Stephan sputtered. "If there was ever a time not to get lost in petty shit, this is it."

"Are you agreeable with me remaining?" Jeremiah asked Renee.

She nodded once, curtly. "Stephan speaks true. I don't like you, nor do I trust you, but everyone else here seems to. It's good enough for me."

He winced at her brash judgment of him but settled into the one remaining chair. For a healer, she didn't bother to sugarcoat how she felt, but then neither had Ronnie, the eagle who'd pulled his bacon out of the fire.

"This won't take long." Renee picked up the mug in front of her and slugged back a goodly portion of its contents. "I was careless. Vampires trapped me."

"Trapped as in cut off your ability to teleport?" Niall broke in.

Renee nodded. "They used mage magic"—she leveled grim green eyes at Niall—"to sully the ley lines' energy. It snared me. First, it forced me out of the air and into my body, and then it formed a perimeter I couldn't break through."

Stephan whistled long and low. "Damn. They're growing stronger."

"No reason they shouldn't," Renee shot back. "They're holding a bunch of mages captive with their magical centers forced open. They take what they want when they want."

Jeremiah had instructed himself to listen. Just listen, but he fisted a hand and brought it down on the table hard enough to make the bottle and glasses rattle. "Cocky fuckers. Serves them right."

"Who?" Renee asked coolly. "The vamps or your kinsmen?"

"They may share blood with me, but I do not call them kinsmen." Jeremiah bristled. He wouldn't dignify her jibe with further commentary.

"How'd you escape?" Sarai asked, inserting the question fast, before Renee could come up with another antagonistic remark.

She tilted her chin defiantly and sat taller in the chair. The motion pushed the mounds of her breasts forward.

Jeremiah couldn't look away, and he hated himself

for giving in to his need to stare. She was more than simply beautiful. With her squared shoulders and the resolute cast to her mouth, she looked like a goddess hellbent on vengeance. Beautiful. Terrible. Indomitable.

He craved her. Yearned to crush her against him and explore her body with mouth and fingers. His cock rose in response to his thoughts, and he was grateful the table shielded his lower body from sight. Niall had said shifters scented arousal, but no one was paying attention to him.

He'd lived alone his whole life. That wasn't about to change. The status quo had always been good enough. It still was. He had plenty on his plate without adding the complications of a new relationship. Especially with a woman who didn't return his interest.

Renee had begun talking, and he focused on her words.

"I escaped because I played to their arrogance. They told me that since they'd tamed mages, turned them into magical cannon fodder, shifters were their next target. They want our animal forms, which totally got my bird spun out."

"I can see where it would have been furious," Stephan said.

"Keep talking." Sarai crooked two fingers in a

come-along gesture. "I still want to know how you outsmarted them."

"They're a bunch of chatty bastards. Told me they could fly, which was why my bird was particularly appealing." She drained her mug, setting it on the table with a clatter. "I challenged them to fly with me, shifted, took to the air, and waited. Two of them took me up on my dare."

This time, it was Jeremiah who whistled. Because he was impressed by her spunk. "Hell, woman, you have brass balls. There are at least half a dozen ways your ploy could have backfired on you. All of them would have meant your death."

"Well, turns out I tossed the dice and won. Enough of their magic was diverted into flight, I was able to grab the offensive and cast a travel spell." She skinned her lips back from her teeth. "If it hadn't, I was fully prepared to kill myself."

"Still carry that ensorcelled dirk, do you?" Stephan narrowed his eyes.

Renee nodded and poured more liquor into her cup. "I do, and I had it clutched in my fist, ready to use. That's about it. A narrow call, but I'm here to fight another day. So's my bird." She turned the full force of her gaze on Jeremiah and added, "My bondmate is not in agreement with your cave lion's plans to take on the vampires. It's another reason we flew away when we did."

He snorted. "Neither is anyone else. I got an earful while you were gone. All good arguments." He pushed to his feet.

"Where do you think you're going?" Stephan asked.

"To discuss this with the other mages. Where else?" He inhaled noisily, blew it out, and gathered his thoughts. "We have a big problem. But it's multifaceted. We have to get rid of the mages who signed up for Vampire boot camp. Once we do that, the vamps will be easier to deal with."

"They may sink back into oblivion," Niall muttered. "No reason for them to be this visible with their usual level of magic. Humans would catch wind of them and out would come the salt and holy water and silver- and lead-laced bullets."

"Regardless," Jeremiah countered. "Step one is locating the mages. Once they're dead—or magicless— they won't be aiding vamps anymore." He transferred his attention to Renee. "Your captors didn't happen to mention how many mages were involved, did they?"

She shook her head. "I should have asked, but I was focused on getting away."

"They might not have told you anyway." Sarai patted Renee's hand. "You're staying with us."

"And we're staying together," Niall said, his tone chilly and determined.

"Which means you're taking a risk if you leave, and it's not wise," Stephan said to Jeremiah.

"Noted. But I'm not going to cower here until we come up with a solution."

"We're not cowering. We're being prudent." Stephan sounded annoyed.

"Fine. I'll be prudent in Silverthorne. My kin have a right to know all of this, and it's not a conversation I want to trust to either telepathy or my cell phone." He nodded brusquely. "I'll contact you and sooner rather than later. I have the beginnings of a plan in place to locate the mages the vamps are extracting power from."

"What is it?" Niall asked.

"Yes. We can help," Sarai chimed in.

Jeremiah held up both hands, palms outward. "I need to run it past the other mages, first."

"'Tisn't mage versus shifter, mate. Not anymore." Niall's words could have etched glass.

"Never said it was." Jeremiah turned and hurried through the door and into the yard. He recognized situations where there was no winning, and this was one of them. His magic straddled two worlds, or maybe the magical strain powering both mages and shifters had finally come full circle and the two were about to become one again.

The door banged behind him. "Hold up for a moment," Sarai called.

He turned to face her. "Apologies, but I have to do things in my own way. It's—"

"Not why I'm out here," she cut him off. "I'm going into town to my shop. I'm certain Niall will come with me, but that part isn't important. I'll be finetuning your chart and researching my source books. I'm the local repository for shifter lore materials, mostly because no one else wanted them."

Jeremiah waited. She had a point, but it wasn't obvious. When she didn't add to her explanation, he asked, "Why tell me?"

She ran lightly down the porch steps to where he stood. "More courtesy than anything else. Don't mind Renee. She's spooked and casting about for a scapegoat. She'll get over it."

"Or not."

Sarai raked her red hair away from her face. "I'll call you if I find anything interesting. When will you be back here?"

"I wasn't necessarily planning to come back."

She chewed her lower lip, nostrils flaring with tension. "I don't want to overreach myself before I check a few things, but we'll need a common launching point for our offensive." Sarai paused for emphasis. "An offensive that includes mages and shifters, which is why you returning is important. We'll have to meet somewhere."

He'd come to the same conclusion but was reluctant to include his kinsmen without talking with them and reaching a consensus. It was how they governed themselves: by discussion and democratic process.

"I understand, but I cannot speak for the others. Not my housemates in Silverthorne or the other mages scattered through this region."

"Go. Do what you need to. We'll be in touch."

"Thanks for believing in me." He gritted his teeth. "Renee is probably convinced I'm on my way to sell all of you out to the highest bidder."

Sarai patted his arm. "Like I said. She's upset. She'll get over it."

The screen slammed, and Niall trotted across the porch and into the yard, a set of car keys dangling from one hand. "Stephan said to take the truck. You ready to leave?"

"Sure. After we offload what's left of your stuff from the bed."

Niall groaned. "Hadn't exactly forgotten about it, but we didn't quite finish that project, now did we?"

Sarai angled an indulgent glance his way and hustled to the back of the truck where she grabbed a box, set if off to one side, and returned for another.

"Let us know you made it home in one piece, eh, mate?" Niall punched Jeremiah lightly in the shoulder before joining Sarai.

"Do you need help?" Jeremiah asked.

"Nah," Sarai replied. "Not all that much left."

"I should know. I helped pack everything," he retorted. "Sure you couldn't use an extra set of hands?"

"Nope. Get moving. Sooner we get our ducks in a row, the sooner we can tackle those renegade mages." Niall dropped a box, offered a thumbs up sign, and went back to unpacking.

Jeremiah strode to the Vette. Once inside, he fired the engine and guided the low-slung car down Stephan's long driveway and out onto the interstate. His mind was full of Renee. Her luxuriant hair. Her shrewd green eyes that glittered like emeralds but could darken to a deep, mossy patina. Her long legs and curvy hips. When he recreated what her breasts looked like, the outline of her nipples stark against the thin fabric of her shirt, he drew himself up short.

His cock was achingly hard. So distended, his breath came fast. He hadn't touched himself in months, but now wasn't the time to remedy his sexless existence. He had bigger problems than his libido that had jumped its bounds and grabbed center stage.

To divert himself, he focused on his bondmate. "You've been quiet."

"I made a mistake choosing you to bond with. You sold me out."

Shock poured over his head like a bucket of ice-cold water. "Uh, I can see how you might feel that way." He stumbled over the words, feeling blindsided. The last thing he needed was one more problem to deal with. A roar blasted out of him, reverberating through the car.

"Stop that!"

"Why should I? You stood by while the other shifters ripped holes in my orders. You're my bondmate. It means you support me."

Jeremiah took a measured breath. Should he have this conversation while driving? He could take things slow and see how they went. If he turned into a menace on the freeway, he could always pull to the shoulder.

He aimed for logic and a cool head before saying, "I can support you and not agree with how you want to proceed."

Another roar. This one so loud it made his ears ache.

"Not how things work," the cave lion shouted. *"The other animals owe allegiance to me. Your job is to ensure they do as I instruct."*

"Even if it appears your marching orders are ill advised?" He winced. He should have quested about for a more diplomatic way of posing the question. Anticipating the lion's ire, he signaled and pulled to the shoulder, killing both his engine and his lights.

He considered stepping outside the Vette but settled for pushing the passenger door open in case the lion forced a shift. He waited, but the beast was silent. He felt it close to the surface, though, restless and pacing.

Not knowing if it was the right thing to do, he said, "We're new to one another. I know almost nothing about shifter magic, but nor do you understand how I wield power. We could help one another."

"What do you have that I could possibly need?" the lion sneered, but at least it wasn't commandeering his vocal cords to roar.

"Knowledge. I've been living in this world. You've been...elsewhere."

"Even assuming I agreed with you—and I don't—all your knowledge didn't keep others with your brand of power from selling out to our common enemy."

Anger bubbled hot. So much for a rational approach.

"You're treating me just like Renee did. Assuming because a few mages were rotten turncoats, all of us are." Fueled by ire he'd shoved aside during his time across the table from Renee, he kept on rolling. "You knew I was a mage when you bonded with me—

without my consent. You knew about the vampire problem—and the mage power fueling it, yet you chose me to bond with. Why? Did you assume I'd be some tractable minion you could bend to your will?"

"Of course not. I selected you because your strength complements mine."

Jeremiah blew out a frustrated breath. "Part of having strength is thinking independently. You can't have it both ways. Either you pick someone weak and obedient—if you want a yes-man. Or you select a worthy partner who won't always agree with you.

"If you're convinced bonding with me was a mistake, undo it, but figure out which horse you're going to ride now. I'm not going to live with you threatening to decamp every time something happens you don't like."

A rich rumble filled his chest, making his breastbone vibrate. It took a moment before he realized the cave lion was purring. *"I like you. I didn't want to after what happened earlier, but it appears my instincts choosing you weren't as far off course as I feared."*

"We're partners, right?" Jeremiah sought clarification.

Another purr clinched his impression. He shut the passenger door and guided the Vette back into light traffic. He hadn't been bonded long, but the lion's absence would have left an empty space. He quested about for words to tell his bondmate he was glad it wasn't leaving, but maybe the lion knew without the awkwardness of conversation.

He hoped so. While the beast continued to purr, he thought about how to approach the other mages. He wasn't concerned about their courage, but he had to prepare them for a less than rosy welcome from at least some of the shifters. Not that it would be a surprise to the small group he lived with. They'd been there when Niall did a hatchet job on all of them because of Jeremiah's actions.

A few shifters accepted them now, but bad blood ran deep between their people. What would it take to meld them into a cohesive team again? Something more than people forced into fighting on the same side in a war none of them wanted.

CHAPTER 6

"Do you mind if I go into town with Niall and Sarai?" Renee asked Stephan, worried about leaving the mountain lion shifter alone.

"Too antsy to sit still, eh?"

She nodded. "Yeah. I'll calm down faster if I have something to do."

He pushed to his feet. "We'll all go. I have errands I need to run."

"Thanks." Gratitude welled, adding to the myriad emotions buffeting her.

"It's okay. Better than sitting here stewing in adrenaline and hoping a bunch of vamps show up so I can behead them."

An eagle's hunting cry burst from Renee, and she grinned. "My bondmate likes your style."

Stephan was already out the door, yelling for the others to wait for them.

She snatched a black wool cloak from a hook next to the door and wrapped it around herself. She was cold, and it wasn't the kind of chill sitting in a warm car would fix. She'd been in a heated house, and her teeth were still on the edge of chattering. Glancing about, she located her purse and slung it over one shoulder.

Even before she came to the States, she'd never had quite as up close and personal an interaction with vampires as what she'd just lived through. Generally, they avoided anyone with magic who might reveal them to unsuspecting humans. One thing was certain. They'd be furious she'd bested them and out for vengeance. They had the feel of her, the smell of her, and they wouldn't rest until they evened today's score.

"Renee!" Stephan's voice was sharp. "Even if you're having second thoughts, you can't stay here by yourself."

She hurried out the door, twisting the lock before shutting it. "Tell me something I don't know," she muttered as she ran to a large, sturdy farm truck with the engine idling and a pile of boxes sitting nearby. It was one of the double-cab models, and she slid into the back seat. As an afterthought, she dug her keys out of her shoulder bag and hit the clicker to lock her SUV.

No reason to make it easy for the vamps to fuck with her.

She waited until they were underway before saying, "Anyone in proximity to me will be in danger. I'll go with you into town, but once we return, I'm leaving."

"You can't do that," Sarai protested.

"You'll be a sitting duck," Niall broke in. "We can't allow it."

Renee bristled. "I'm a free agent. I'll do what I need to. Vampires are exceptional trackers. They'll come after me because of today, and not just four of them. They'll send an entire fucking army."

Insidious cold spread from her stomach outward until it felt like she was encased in a block of ice. "I'll take my bird form. I'll be harder to find that way, especially if I lose myself in a flock of eagles."

"Where were you planning to find them?" Niall asked.

"Southeast Alaska," she retorted. "It will take me time to fly there, which should get me off their radar too. I can't go home, and anyone around me will be in serious jeopardy."

Sarai sat between Stephan who was driving and Niall. In a graceful move, she turned until she was perched on her knees facing Renee. Her lovely face was set in grim lines. "I've never known you to be a coward."

The words stung. "I'm not a coward," Renee sputtered. "I'm doing this so they don't take you down with me."

Sarai shook her head until hair fell into her eyes. "Doesn't work that way. We need every shifter to fight. If you throw your life away, all it means is one less soldier on our side."

"If I remain with other shifters, it may mean a whole lot more deaths than one less soldier," she countered.

"We did a fair job fighting twenty vamps in that Eastern European castle we ended up in thanks to Jeremiah's misguided scheme," Niall spoke up.

"He was incredibly brave and resourceful." Sarai shot a pointed look at her mate.

"I know you think that, sweetheart, but he could have gotten us all killed."

"What did he do?" Renee asked.

"Compelled their healer to concoct a slow-acting poison—slow for mages, that is. Once he had it on board, he coaxed eighteen vamps to drink from him before he collapsed," Niall replied.

"Whatever it was, the poison was far more toxic to the vampires, and they burned up from the inside out,"

Sarai said, adding, "I took my wolf form and jumped two more, who were trying to escape."

"I thought only silver and iron bullets, or beheading, would kill them," Renee muttered.

"Same thing I thought," Stephan said, "but I was wrong."

Renee turned the information over. Jeremiah told her he'd been gravely ill and healed by a shifter. "Was it one of us who made sure the poison didn't kill him too?"

Sarai nodded. "Yes, another eagle shifter, Ronnie. You might know him."

"I do. He's a good man. In truth, he's a distant relative. All of us have the healing knack. Do we know why Jeremiah risked his skin?"

"Aye." Niall glanced over a shoulder. "He meant to set an example for the mages who'd signed on with the dark side."

"Huh? How so?" Renee frowned, not connecting the dots.

"His approach was twofold," Niall went on. "It rid the world of a decent number of vamps and also sent a message to the mages who were strengthening vampire power."

"Indeed," Stephan chimed in. "The implication was they'd be our next targets."

Renee chewed her lower lip. "If what the vampires

told me today is true, the mages no longer have a choice in the matter. They're shackled by vamp mesmerism, providing a ready source of magic."

"Serves them right. If they had a shred of decency left, they'd refuse food and water until they had no more power for the vamps to siphon." Niall's tone was dark.

"For all we know, the vampires are forcing blood on them and they're in limbo, neither mage nor vampire, but some no-man's land in between," Stephan muttered.

"Aye, 'twould certainly downplay their need for nourishment," Niall said.

Sarai leveled her gaze at Renee. "You're not going off on your own. It's not up for discussion." Before Renee could reply, she turned back around.

No one seemed inclined to talk further as the truck sped toward Denver on the interstate. Eventually, Stephan turned off onto city streets. The small respite offered thinking time. Even though she hated to offer Jeremiah points for anything, she was impressed by his courage. He'd been willing to die to prove a point.

She reminded herself the bond animals were almost never wrong. According to her eagle, the lion had searched long and hard for a shifter to bond with. That it picked Jeremiah suggested the mage—shifter, she corrected herself—had significant worth.

Yeah, and I treated him like warmed-over dogmeat.

She cringed. Maybe she'd get a chance to apologize, but for now she needed a game plan. The vamps would be all over her no matter what she did to divert them. Hiding behind wards wouldn't do it. Besides, she couldn't maintain extreme warding 24/7. It would drain her magic over a couple of days and she'd need time to recover.

Time when she was unwarded and vulnerable.

Stephan turned the truck down an alleyway and parked.

"You're coming inside with us," Sarai said to her uncle.

"Eventually. For now, I'm going to drop you off and drive to the feedstore. I have to inform the others about today."

"We can use telepathy for that, Uncle," Sarai protested. Dark circles sat beneath her eyes, and her forehead was creased into a welter of fine lines.

"How?" Stephan turned to face her. "We share our magical origins with mages. They're capable of eavesdropping on our telepathy. Presumably vamps can as well. Cellular calls are easy for anyone without any power at all to hack. The feedstore is only about fifteen minutes away. I'll be back here long before you're done."

Sarai gave her uncle a quick hug. "Keep your psychic view peeled."

"Oh believe me, I plan to. Out, everyone. I'll return as soon as I can."

Niall opened the passenger door and jumped down, offering a hand to Sarai. Renee exited from the closest rear door and reached back inside to grab her shoulder bag. For the first time ever, she wished for a gun. And silver-and-lead laced bullets. Magic killed, but you had to be close to your targets. Guns offered a safety margin, one where you didn't risk being snared by vampire mind control.

She slammed her door and hurried after the other two shifters. She'd visited Sarai's shop a time or two. The place always smelled divine from all the dried herbs and flowers Sarai used to create decoctions and potions.

Still antsy as hell, feeling naked and exposed, she scanned with magic and hissed, "Stop."

Niall and Sarai turned as a unit. "Why?" Sarai asked.

Renee whispered, "I smell vampire."

Sarai hooked a hand beneath her arm. "It's old. They were here, but they're not now. Believe me, I know the difference."

"They attacked you here?" Renee could scarcely get the words out.

"Yeah. My own fault. I wasn't careful, but I was holding my own until Stephan showed up. Then things went downhill fast."

"Until I got there," Niall growled. "Come on you two. We can chew the fat inside."

Renee had questions. Lots of them, but she bit her tongue. Recent events weren't nearly as important as what came next. They had a lot of planning to do. Once they were inside and Niall had wrapped a ward around the office, she said, "I'm not worth much with astrological stuff, but I want to help."

Sarai trotted to an overflowing bookshelf and dug three fat tomes out from beneath a stack of slightly thinner volumes. "You can work on the lore part. Start with these," she instructed.

"What am I looking for?"

"Anything in our histories that addresses vampires or mages gone rogue."

Renee took the books and settled on an overstuffed leather couch. Sarai booted up her computer and began typing.

"Give me one of those." Niall sat on the other side of the couch. "Looks like it will take forever to cull through them."

She handed him a book. "If these operate like other shifter lore books, they're scarcely indexed. Open your magical center and ask them a question. They should point to something useful. If they don't, finetune your query until it yields what you're looking for."

"Exactly," Sarai said without turning around. Her fingers flew over the keys, and images danced across her screen.

"It's never the book's fault," Niall muttered and opened the volume lying atop his lap. The smells of old parchment intensified as he splayed his hands across crinkled pages.

"Pretty much. How could it be?" Renee grinned, feeling more centered than she had since the vampires forced her out of the sky. She switched to the floor and opened both books in front of her, chanting softly. Magic rose and fell around her in varying tones and timbres.

The forthright, masculine tones of Niall's casting blended with the power shimmering around Sarai, turning the air incandescent. The tang of shifter workings filled the cozy office, redolent of forests and oceans and trees wetted down from a brisk rain.

She inhaled hungrily. The metallic scents of modern life—concrete, plastic, chemicals—had all but drowned out the natural world, overshadowing it with phony, crude smells that chipped away at her soul. Shifters had a long, proud history. She felt humbly fortunate to be counted among their numbers.

Pages riffled beneath her fingers, slow at first and

then faster. The question she'd asked was what role she and her eagle played in the unexpected rise of vampire power. Normally, she had to ask a dozen questions. She'd never hit the nail on the head first time off the blocks.

She took it as a good omen.

Or maybe a very bad one.

The pages of the book on her left stopped abruptly. A few leaves flipped back the other way. She could have sworn the damned thing was glowing, so she switched to her psychic view to check.

Breath whooshed from her. Ley lines wrapped around the tome, glistening in shades of orange and gold. The book was so beautiful, her throat thickened with emotion. When she glanced up to show Niall and Sarai, the room wasn't there. Instead, a thick mist surrounded her.

Panic surged until she understood her own magic had created the cocoon. No vampires. No mages. Just her and her nascent power. The book on the right quieted as well. It hadn't been rustling as fast, so the place it stopped moving didn't require backtracking.

She inhaled raggedly, blew it out, and did it again. Nothing changed. The magic circling her was as sweet and pure as any in her long lifetime. With fingers that trembled a little, she picked up the left-hand book and began to read. Shockwaves rocked her as she skimmed today's events. They weren't perfectly aligned with reality, but close enough.

The book knew what had happened to her.

It detailed the danger mages posed. For some reason, it discounted vamps as scarcely worth anyone's time but stressed that their unholy alliance with mages would make them more dangerous by a factor of a thousand. A chill tracked down her spine, all sharp claws and teeth, a feral animal on the loose with her as its target.

When she turned one more page, it was blank.

Renee licked dry lips. She'd been here before. This book had run its course. She'd have to feed it another question to cull more from its pages. She ran a few possibilities through her mind since the book hadn't told her anything she didn't already know.

The other book edged toward her with a slithering, slapping noise. Her eyes widened, and she stretched a hand to pick it up, placing it atop the first. She'd never known lore books could move, but if their pages could turn independently, anything was possible. She focused on the indicated page.

It blurred, the letters rearranging themselves in a crazy, arcane ballet as she watched. Many languages showed up in the lore books. The one taking shape before her was a form of ancient Gaelic. Except when she'd learned it, it had been called old Gaelic, not ancient.

Her mind was wandering, and she had a prickly feeling at the base of her spine. The cozy cocoon around her hadn't changed, and she was still shrouded by silvery mist. The others couldn't be worried about her, or they'd be trying to break through.

As soon as the letters stopped jumping around, she began to read. After the first sentence or two, her heart skipped into triple-time rhythm, pounding so hard she feared it would beat right through her chest. The premise laid out before her was so fantastic, it was impossible to believe.

But the books never lied.

She read the two pages twice, looked for more, and came up with the same blank vellum she'd found in the first book. Her fingertips tingled where they contacted the page. Because she was still tuned into her psychic view, she saw the ley lines disentangle themselves from the books, one at a time. Once the second one was free, the mist pooled into iridescent strands that melted into the ether.

Sarai was still at her keyboard. Niall hadn't moved from his spot on the sofa. He shook a fist at his book and raked a hand through his dark hair.

Not knowing quite where to begin, Renee cleared her throat.

"Yes, hon?" Sarai asked, adding, "Give me a minute. I'm nearly done, and brother is this a game changer, but you may not like it much."

"Good you came up with something," Niall muttered. "So far I've hit one dry hole after the next." He shook his head. "Never been much of one for books, and this is why. They hate me."

"Aw, sweetie." Sarai not only turned around, she got up and went to Niall, giving him a hug. "Take a little break and try a different one. They're keyed to different wavelengths. Maybe that's not the book for you."

"Bollocks. None of them ever are," he said sourly.

Renee got to her feet, bones cracking as she stretched out the kinks. "What was that about a game changer?" Before Sarai could answer, she blurted, "Uh, did either of you notice anything strange about me?"

Sarai offered a lopsided grin. "Is that a general, open-ended question?"

"Aye because the lass has always been a wee bit on the eccentric side." Niall winked.

Renee rolled her shoulders back. "I wasn't exactly here this past little while." A quick glance at a wall clock suggested half an hour had ticked by.

"What do you mean, not here?" Niall's smile faded. "By all the gods, woman, you were sitting in the same place on the floor while I cursed my book from front to back."

"No wonder it refused you knowledge," Sarai mumbled.

"I didn't begin by cursing it." Niall rolled his eyes. "Even I know better than to antagonize magical accoutrements."

Before the two of them sidetracked into a theoretical discussion about how to coax power into action, Renee jumped in and said, "My magic, it built a shelter around me. Both books were extremely responsive. When I looked with my third eye, their energy had joined with the ley lines, and the whole thing pulsed and throbbed. It wasn't unpleasant. Rather like being in a magical cave."

"What happened then?" Sarai's question held tense edges.

"The first book was a replay of what transpired with the vamps today. At least according to the book, vamps on their own are mostly a nuisance, but them joining up with mages is a fucking disaster."

The door flew inward, and Stephan joined them. "I heard that last part," he bellowed. "What I want to know is if the three of you came up with something we don't already know." He kicked the door shut behind him.

Breath hissed through Renee's teeth, her first clue

she'd clenched her jaws. Here it was. Rubber-meeting-road time. "Um yeah." She faced Stephan. "Apparently, it wasn't sheer bad luck—wrong place, wrong time—behind my abduction. I'm linked with Jeremiah in ways I can't totally wrap my mind around, and we were together before the vamps zeroed in on me. If I'd remained with him, none of it would have happened."

She was babbling, but she couldn't stem the flow of words. "See, it wasn't accidental he hatched up that plan to kill the vamps, either. Everything is part of this huge gameboard, with the strategies already mapped out—except we don't fully know what they are. He and I are supposed to team up, work together. Without our joined energies, the vamps will win."

When she looked at the others, Sarai was nodding, a somber expression on her face. "Matches up with what I saw in his chart. And yours."

"What were you doing mucking around in my chart?" Renee's voice held a shrill note she didn't care much for, but she couldn't seem to modulate it.

Sarai shrugged. "Call it intuition. It's how my magic works. I dug deeper into his chart, saw some gaps I was certain your chart would provide complements for, and went for it. Synastry in action."

"That's the game changer part?" Renee asked.

"Yup. Turns out your Aquarius is an almost perfect

mating for his Leo. The energy the two of you could unleash would be enough to change any world, not just mitigate the vampire problem."

"Whew. That's a lot to absorb," Niall said. "Maybe we should get your mum back here—to doublecheck the astrology parts."

"I do not need my mother for that." Sarai sounded pissed with a definite edge to her tone.

"Sure and I wasn't meaning to discount your skills, darling." Niall got to his feet and wrapped an arm around his mate. "But before we go shoving two folk who aren't seemingly too fond of one another together, we'll want to make certain 'tis the proper course."

Renee stood tall. "My book intimated he and I needed to work together, not that we were necessarily mates."

"That's why it's useful to have more than one magical stream in play." Sarai smiled benignly. "You can fight it all you want, but you two are destined for one another. Remember. A shifter's mate is in the stars."

"I've never believed that, and I am not letting you run my life. Or ruin it, for that matter." Renee turned away from her friend, wanting to strangle her. "If you're not ready to leave, I'm teleporting back to my car."

"The hell you are." Niall glowered from where he stood next to Sarai.

"Who's going to give the groom—er, Jeremiah—the news?" Stephan asked.

"No one!" Renee shrieked. "There's no groom. No bride. No fucking mates. If any of you open your mouths about this, I will leave. And you'll never, ever be able to find me."

"Aye. Because you'll be dead." Niall let go of Sarai and dropped a hand onto Renee's shoulder. "We have enough problems without you turning into a prima donna. Pull yourself together. Now."

"We're going home. We all could use food and rest." Stephan's voice was gruff. "Things will look better after a night's sleep."

Renee let them herd her out of Sarai's shop. The way things were shaping up, things wouldn't ever be better. One of the big plusses about the twenty-first century was no arranged matings. Women could be unmated if they chose. Or sleep around. Or have two or three mates—at the same time.

She settled into the back seat again. Anger traded turns with resignation, but her eyes kept closing. Somewhere between Denver and Stephan's ranch, she fell into an exhausted sleep.

CHAPTER 7

"Oooh. Shift for me!" Chloe danced around Jeremiah, bouncing with enthusiasm. Her unbound hair swirled around her looking like burnished gold. Tall and broad-shouldered for a woman, she wore an ancient pair of black running shorts and a long-sleeved blue shirt blazoned with, *Magic Rocks, Live the Dream* in hot pink lettering edged with silver gilt.

He leveled stern eyes on his sister. "Stop it. Shifting isn't for showing off or airing a performance." He tucked a hand beneath her upper arm and spun her so she faced him. "I didn't ask for this. It came to me unbidden."

"Yes, but why?" Her blue eyes glowed with keen interest.

"Not sure. Probably has something to do with that eagle shifter who healed me."

Chloe narrowed her eyes and tilted her head to one side. "Our magic shares common roots with shifter power. If what I've read is correct, mages could shift too, a very long time ago. I have no idea why our ability took a different road, but it did. Except maybe that phase is behind us." She clasped her hands together. "I'm going to do everything I can to attract my own bondmate."

Jeremiah's heart hurt for his twin sister. She'd spent much of their childhood playing with a series of imaginary animals. First a bear, then a wolf, and finally a coyote. He wanted to be supportive but needed to redirect her energies, so he said, "I'm impressed by your knowledge. You're far better versed in our history than I am, but how about relegating your shifter project to a back burner? Not forever, but for now."

"Hmmm. I know that tone. Means you have something you want me to do." She crooked two fingers his way. "Out with it."

He hastily sketched out what he'd discovered about the captive mages who'd moved from voluntary recruits to prisoners.

Chloe's smile faded, replaced by a harsh expression. "Too bad for them, but nothing those bastards don't deserve. I can see the problem, though.

So long as they're detained, they're providing fodder for vamps to use as they will." She slithered out from beneath his grip. "What will we do when we find them?"

He exhaled noisily and winced. "Good question. The prudent course would be to kill them, but maybe they'll be ready to see reason and—"

"Nope." Chloe shook her head emphatically. "You're an old softie. You always have been."

"I am not." He bristled at the implication and started to launch into the difference between compassion and stupidity, but Chloe wasn't done.

"Be that as it may," she hurried on, "we can't take the chance. They turned on us once. They could do the same thing again. For all we know, something about their time with the vamps might make them more susceptible to vampire coercion."

He offered her points for quick thinking. "Maybe you're right. Vampires are good trackers, which means they could locate the mages without much effort. If they can find them, then they'd find us, and—"

"I knew you'd see it my way," she broke in. "Do you have any idea where to start looking?" She headed toward the stairs.

"Yes, I do. Where are you going?"

"To change clothes. We're leaving immediately, right?"

"Hold up there, sister. We're not doing this alone. I want to include as many mages as want to ride along. Shifters too."

Chloe turned at the foot of the stairwell until she faced him. "What are you now? One of us? Or one of them?"

He thought back to Niall's terse pronouncement about it no longer being an us and them proposition. Not anymore. He met his sister's direct gaze. "I'm me. Just as I've always been. I wield magic, and now I have an alternative form. We have to move past our residual antagonism toward shifters. If we don't play on the same team, things won't go well for us, and the vampires might win."

She looked as if she'd bitten into something bitter. "There was a time when we said the same thing about shifters. That if we didn't remain at the top of our game, they'd overtake us."

"I know. Hard feelings take a long time to resolve, and there were a whole lot of them up until very recently. In truth, there still are. They haven't gone away—on either side." He stood straighter, remembering Renee's antagonism toward him. "Do you have any idea when everyone will be back?"

"An hour or so, maybe less. They went out to dinner."

"How come you didn't go with them?"

She shrugged. "I was worried about you. If you hadn't shown up when you did, I was going to track you with magic and go after you."

He smiled crookedly. It was good to be cared about, but she was being way too overprotective. "Thanks. I'm going to do a little digging between now and when the others return. Check on my theory about where the mages are being held."

"Not by yourself, you're not."

"Oberon's balls, woman. This will be dangerous. Definitely a job for one person. I have a far better chance getting in and out unnoticed on my own."

She stood tall. "It damn near killed me when you went off alone with all that poison on board. I stayed strong because I didn't want to make your decision harder than it was, but I swore if a miracle happened and you returned alive, I was never swallowing my reservations again."

Chloe strode to him, covering the distance fast. "Two choices, bud. Either you bring me, or I'll use magic to pinpoint your location and come anyway."

"I can bind you, force you to remain here."

She furled her brows. "Try it. You might have a surprise or two in store."

Fire sparked from her gaze, and Jeremiah stared hard at the grim-faced woman he thought he knew. Chloe was usually agreeable. When had that changed?

"About two hundred years ago." She snorted. "Yeah, I was inside your mind. You've always treated me like a kid sister. It was convenient to have you underestimate me. Made my life simpler when I needed to slip something past you, but I'm over it."

He started to ask which things she'd deployed beneath his radar but closed his jaws with an audible *clack*. Now wasn't the time for a family squabble, and no matter what she said, he was certain he'd be furious. "Fine. I'll start a travel spell brewing. Be back downstairs in five minutes."

Chloe slugged him in the shoulder almost hard enough to hurt before bounding out of the room and up the stairs. She'd won and knew better than to ruin her victory with words.

He opened a channel to his power, chanting softly. Magic bubbled around him, iridescent and pregnant with promise. The lion's presence added a significant boost to his ability. Spells came easier—a whole lot easier.

Immersed in his own casting, he was slow to notice other magic nipping at the edges of his spell.

"We have company," the lion informed him.

Jeremiah's head snapped up. His bondmate hadn't suggested they'd need to defend themselves, but the fact it had to say anything at all was worrisome. He gritted his teeth. Nowhere was safe. He wasn't in the habit of being vigilant in his home, but that had to change.

Once he refocused beyond the edges of his travel spell, he picked up the distinct magical tang of shifters. Before he could sort out who was almost upon him, Niall, Sarai, Stephan, and Renee shimmered into focus on the far side of the room.

"At least you guessed right about his location." Renee sounded as sour and out of sorts as she had earlier.

"I did not *guess*." Niall's response was pointed.

"No, you wouldn't have had to," Jeremiah agreed, using words to cover his surprise at the impromptu visit. "You've been here before."

"We didn't expect to find you," Stephan said, "but Niall convinced us to begin here, so we could track whatever path your magic left."

"Who's here?" Chloe called, followed by, "Never mind. I figured it out." Her footsteps clattering down the stairs coincided with the last of her words. She'd put on scuffed boots, dark trousers, and a black, hooded jacket zipped to her chin. "Nice to see all of you again." Chloe nodded pleasantly at the shifters and held a hand out to Renee. "I'm Chloe, Jeremiah's twin."

Renee shook her hand and replied, "I'm Renee."

"We got here in time." Niall directed his comment to Stephan.

"In time for what?" Jeremiah kept the question bland.

Niall rolled his eyes and crossed to where Jeremiah stood. "For the love of the Fae, man, we're on the same team. You have suspicions about where the mages are being held. Judging from the feel of the magic bouncing around this room, you were about to leave to search for them."

Jeremiah opened his mouth to deny it, but his bondmate spoke up. *"Not a good idea. Allies hold no secrets."*

"At least your bondmate has decent instincts," Renee snarled. Dark circles sat beneath her eyes. She looked like she could do with an uninterrupted night's rest and a few square meals.

"You're trashed." He didn't mince words. "You should go home and get some sleep."

"None of us will remain by ourselves. Not after what happened to Renee this morning." Sarai skewered him with her blue eyes. "We didn't think you should have left, either."

Chloe had let go of Renee's hand, but she still stood near the eagle shifter. "What happened this morning?"

"It's an unpleasant story. The short version is I wasn't paying attention and ended up captured by a passel of vampires." Renee sucked in a tight breath. "Now they're out for my blood."

"Damn! I'm sorry." Chloe nodded briskly. "Good thinking on your part to outfox them."

Engines rumbled as cars pulled into the driveway. Jeremiah reorganized his priorities. His nice, clean, secret reconnaissance was off the table. With all of them here, they could launch a raid, but it would get side railed once he told them about the lion.

"Listen up," he said. "Once my housemates are inside, we're going to plan an offensive to locate and destroy the captured mages. I want us to be on our way in short order, though, so it would be best if you didn't mention my lion."

A long, rumbling snarl burst from his mouth. Apparently, his bondmate didn't think much of his plan. "We need to get moving." He directed his comment to the lion. "It's been hours since Renee conned the vampires. They'll be on the move soon, if they aren't already. If we tell everyone I'm a shifter, they may not trust me. We can't afford to blow an hour —let alone three or four—talking this through. I promise I'll tell them—it's not something I'm ashamed of—but I'll do it afterward."

Another growl ripped through him. He tensed. Would the lion force its way out again? Not much he could do about it. The beast's power trumped his.

Voices drifted from outside; the front door flew open.

"Jeremiah!" a slender, dark-haired man named Johnny exclaimed. "Good to see you. You've been spending so much time with shifters, we've been worried you sold out to the dark side."

"See what I mean?" Jeremiah told his bondmate, switching to telepathy. He braced for the roar that would give him away, but it never materialized.

Stephan turned the full force of his tall, burly presence on Johnny and glowered.

A thread of magic flared from Johnny as he assessed Stephan's brand of power; his eyes widened. "Um, no harm no foul. I misspoke." He tugged a denim jacket closer around his spare frame.

"For the love of the goddess, don't compound things with a lie." Jeremiah sharpened his tone. "We have a problem, and it's not shifters. I was with our 'dark side' cousins earlier today dealing with it." He took a measured breath. "Some of you know Stephan, Niall, and Sarai." He pointed at them as he said their names. "You haven't met Renee yet."

Liam, one of the oldest of them, hastened toward her, arms extended. "I remember you from before we crossed the sea—and before the war. It's good to see you."

"Good to see you too." She hugged the white-haired mage, and a quick, hot pang of jealousy caught Jeremiah square in the chest.

A murmur of names rolled through the room as the mages extended introductions. Five of them, including Chloe, had been with Jeremiah when they'd hidden in a deserted mining town. That had been when he'd played sacrificial goat with his poison scheme.

"Now that we all know one another," Jeremiah cut in, "our task is to locate a group of imprisoned mages. Things are far worse than we thought. Out mage kin are no longer free. Vampires have mesmerized them and are siphoning their power. We must cut their source off at the roots."

"Cut it off, how?" Mariel, a red-haired mage, asked in a strangled=sounding voice.

"By killing them," Chloe said. "Jer and I argued about it earlier, but we can't take a chance on leaving any of them alive."

"Normally, I wouldn't agree." Raul, their healer, stepped forward. "But in this case, I do." Tawny hair shot with gray fell to his shoulders, and his hazel eyes glittered with keen intelligence and determination.

Niall offered a grin that was all teeth and zero warmth. "Good use for us dark-siders. Keeps the blood off your hands."

"We're going to free them only to kill them?" Johnny spoke up.

"Aye, why bother to free them at all?" Mariel's words were tough, but her brown eyes pinched with worry at their corners.

"If we leave them where they are, the vampires will be able to turn them," Sarai replied.

"Not if they're dead," Mariel protested.

"Vampires are dead," Raul reminded her. "If they find the mages soon enough after death, they can drain and resurrect them."

"'Tis a sure bet they'd locate them in time," Niall put in. "They'll notice right away that the spigot they've been leeching magic from was shut off."

"Do we know how many mages?" Chloe asked.

"Not exactly," Jeremiah replied. "We number fourteen. It would be ideal if we could team up, two to a captive mage, but—"

"Nay," Niall spoke over him. "You need us to do the killing, so once we locate the blackguards, we'll cast a group transport spell."

"And move them where?" Jeremiah asked.

"Good question," Stephan muttered. "How about Golddust?"

Johnny narrowed his dark eyes in thought. "Must be that ghost town you used as a base to launch the last vampire attack."

"That's exactly what it is." Chloe nodded. "It's where we gathered before Jer went vampire hunting."

"As good a choice as any." Jeremiah added his two cents' worth. "It's deserted and off the beaten path. Once we're done, we can burn the bodies, purify them of their misdeeds."

"Or leave them for the crows." Chloe sent a sharp look his way.

"Not our way," he informed her. "If they can find the peace in death that eluded them in life, we have no right to rob them of it."

"Eh. They had no right to choose the undead as playmates," another mage called from near the front door. I'm with Chloe. Leave the fuckers to rot."

"Once they're beyond where vampires can resurrect them," Raul added, an uncharacteristic edge to his tone.

"Where do you think the mages are?" Niall asked pointblank.

Jeremiah had been able to avoid answering him at Stephan's, but every set of eyes in the room was trained on him. He inhaled briskly. "I'm fairly certain it's Mitch and his brothers and cousins. My best guess is they're somewhere near that isolated patch of real estate where they've lived for the last hundred years."

"Do you mean that canyon they teleport into and out of?" Chloe asked.

He nodded and said, "The same," while wondering how she knew about it.

"Where exactly is it?" Niall asked with a slight separation between each word.

"Northern Idaho. Sawtooth Range," Jeremiah answered. "I'm not sure how they found the place, but it's a series of connected caves warmed by geothermal energy. Warm pools. Warm water. Pretty much everything you'd need to be comfortable. The land is rugged, so there aren't any roads. It's the type of place that would appeal to vampires too. Out of the way. Rather like a lair where they could store any number of bodies, feeding from them at their leisure."

"And no one near enough to hear them scream," Johnny added sourly.

"Are we in agreement?" Jeremiah scanned the room. "Worst case scenario, I'm wrong and we'll have to dig deeper to find them."

"Aye, let's get moving." Niall gestured with both hands. "Send me an image of where we're headed."

"What? You don't trust me?" Jeremiah quirked a brow.

"My turn to control the transport spell." Niall's words were mild, without inflection, but Jeremiah understood him well enough. He'd tricked half a dozen shifters into following him to a vampire stronghold, and Niall hadn't forgotten.

"Too many for a single transport spell," Stephan

said. "We'll do best in groups of four to six if we want to maintain stealth when we arrive at the other end."

"Speaking of numbers," Chloe spoke up, "I'm having a hard time remembering just how many family members Mitch had."

"Anywhere from six to ten assorted uncles, brothers, and cousins," Jeremiah answered her. "Depends how many of them voted to become lackeys for vampire central."

"Are all of them men?" Renee asked.

She'd been so quiet, Jeremiah had done a fair job blocking out her presence. It was hard being in the same room with someone who hated him as much as she clearly did. Doubly hard since he was so attracted to her, but he couldn't force her to view him as anything other than a blackguard mage turned shifter by a fortuitous twist of fate.

"Yup, all men," Mariel answered.

Renee turned to face her. "Why? Are they gay?"

Mariel shook her head. "Not a sexual thing. At least I don't believe it was. Mitch didn't care for women."

"Sure, but that's him. How'd he convince a bunch of others to sign on to the same program?" Renee pressed.

"It's not important. His family were always on the odd side. Kept to themselves. We only saw them when they wanted something—even in the Old Country." Jeremiah forced himself to hold eye contact with her. It was hard. She was so goddamned lovely, and she looked so depleted he wanted to gather her close, protect her, keep harm from crossing her threshold ever again.

But she didn't want him. Worse than that, she held him in the same regard she might have for a cockroach.

Renee glanced away. "Yeah. You're right, of course. I'm tired, and it's hard to focus on much of anything."

Surprise rocked him. He hadn't expected her to agree with anything that came out of his mouth. To cover his relief, he blurted, "Form two groups of five and one of four. Niall and Sarai will be in one of the larger groups. Stephan and Renee will pick separate groups. That way, we'll spread the shifters evenly."

Renee scraped her gaze off the floor and stared right at him. He didn't need mindreading to interpret her expression. It fairly screamed he was a shifter just like her, and he was a right bloody coward not to admit it to his mage kin.

He stared back defiantly while the lion paced, restless within him. At least it hadn't outed him, which probably meant it agreed with his assessment that disclosing his status would only get in the way.

"We'll have to move fast when we get there," Stephan was saying. Jeremiah had missed the first part.

"Yeah," Niall agreed. "Once we see how many mages are there, we'll divvy them up, free them, and drag them to Golddust."

"Don't wait on the rest of us once you arrive," Jeremiah cautioned. "Several small transport spells will draw less attention than one huge one."

"No worries on that front." Renee spat the words. "A clean death is too good for them, but it's what they'll get."

The room broke into three groups. Power boiled, hot and viscous, as everyone added their magic to group travel spells.

"Ready." Renee stalked to the far side of Jeremiah's group, taking a place next to Chloe.

His heart beat faster. She'd be with him. How had that happened? Before he could sort it out, the other two groups vanished. He laid everything but the task facing them aside.

"I've got this," he said. "Open your power to me, and we'll be gone in a trice."

$\mathcal{N}$iall and Sarai staked out a spot in one of the larger groups. By the time Renee got to the other group with five—the one without Jeremiah —Stephan was already there. She'd pleaded without words, but he ignored her.

Robbed of choice—other than remaining in the mages' house, which was no choice at all since she had a target painted on her back—she slid in next to Chloe and tilted her chin at a defiant angle. She hadn't wanted to leave Stephan's, had argued vehemently against following Jeremiah.

She'd been outvoted as they stood at the kitchen counter shoveling food down their throats and arguing. It was tough to discount Niall and Sarai, especially after both presented solid points. Niall was convinced Jeremiah would go after the captive mages, and Sarai was worried about him being alone. Stephan said he'd be with other mages but agreed with Niall about the need to not let the trail grow too cold.

Sarai's final nail-in-the-coffin reason had been what Renee had gleaned from the lore book: that her energy needed to be close to Jeremiah's since the combination would protect all of them.

A familiar funny little trill had filled her after she arrived in Jeremiah's living room. No man had a right to be so gorgeous. So appealing. He practically oozed come-fuck-me vibes without even trying. Her heart beat crazily, and the initial attraction that had snared her the first time she laid eyes on him returned with a vengeance. She covered her interest—interest that had zero future—with a gruff comment to Niall about guessing right.

Maybe she could lose herself in killing the turncoat mages. Nothing like a bloodbath to put a damper on lust. The smell of Jeremiah's magic wrapped around her as he cast a travel spell, and she forgot all about killing and blood. Rosemary, vanilla, and rain-wet forests mingled into an enticing mélange, and she was grateful she wasn't near enough to touch him.

She ached to wrap her arms around him, feel the press of his body against hers. Inhaling his scent only intensified her longing. Not breathing wasn't an option, so she did her damnedest to block him out of her mind as the room shimmered into nothingness, replaced by the blackness of their traveling portal.

What if they came out in the wrong place? She'd always kept the upper hand during transport spells. Allowing someone else to control them went against the grain, but Niall had intimated as much too.

Despite her reservations about Jeremiah, she had faith in Chloe. Even though she'd only just met the woman, something genuine about her inspired trust.

Yeah, and she trusts her twin, but this isn't an exercise in inductive reasoning.

"Why are you fighting this?" Her bondmate's question surprised her.

"I'm not. Not exactly. I like being in control. That's all," she responded in shielded telepathy, hoping Jeremiah, Chloe, and the other mage with them, a man named Johnny, wouldn't pick up on her ambivalence.

"Not precisely what I meant. Why do you dislike the idea of him as your mate?"

If the eagle's first question caught her off guard, this next one was a true shocker. She adopted a different tack. *"I thought you were annoyed with the cave lion. Why would you want us to join forces with them?"*

The bird cawed before saying, *"A temporary spat, to be sure. This isn't about the lion and me. It's about you, and you have yet to answer me."*

The air developed the characteristic gray aspect that meant they were closing on their destination. She didn't have to tell her bondmate they needed to look sharp and focus all their attention on what lay in wait for them. Its question would have to wait. A good thing since she didn't have an answer.

Not a good one, anyway. She didn't want to whine about Jeremiah not being interested in her. Nor was she in the mood to look like a pathetic fool by throwing herself at a man who could care less.

The gray surrounding her shaded lighter still. Her muscles tensed, and she peered through the mist, using her psychic view to see better. Ley lines formed, shimmering just as they should. At least the nasty blackened edges hadn't invaded this portion of wherever they were emerging.

If the mages were here, they weren't able to cast magic on their own, or they'd have set a protective perimeter, visible in the lines, to warn them of invaders.

"Almost there." Jeremiah's voice rang in her mind. *"Defensive magic at the ready."*

She almost retorted this was far from her first rodeo, but bit back the comment. He was the closest thing his mage group had to an alpha. The others were probably used to obeying him, and they respected his read on things. She was the outsider.

Not the time to take a stand. Or to earn a reputation as a bitch.

The last strands of mist fell away. They stood in a rugged canyon with walls hundreds of feet tall on both sides. Walls that appeared unscalable without a magical assist. The noise of rushing water filled her ears from a robust river traveling fast only a couple feet away. From the sound of things, a major waterfall wasn't far downstream.

The scent of Jeremiah's power thickened as he searched their location, and she breathed it in.

"This way." He took off at a lope, traversing large, uneven rocks with a fluid grace that earned her respect. Watching his legs pump as they covered distance made her want them wrapped around her.

She tossed cold water on her overheated imagination and picked her way after the others. The terrain was difficult, so she cheated, using magic to ensure she remained on her feet. When she caught up with the others, they stood at the entrance to a large cavern.

"This is the right spot. I remember it," Chloe said.

Jeremiah cast a pointed look her way. "When were you ever here?"

"Doesn't matter. Let's go." She gestured toward the opening and strode through it.

Renee looked away, pleased Chloe wasn't a

milquetoast who'd roll over when her brother ordered her to. She trotted alongside the group as they entered a generous cave. She was still employing her psychic view, and ley lines glowed softly, illuminating the darkness enough for her to pick her way around boulders and limestone formations. Water dripped down the walls, and the place smelled of sulfur from geothermal activity.

A quick scan told her the other mages were close, perhaps in a neighboring cavern. The stench of vampire indicated they were in the right place, but the vamp scents weren't fresh.

Even old vampire spoor made her belly clench with fear and hatred.

A long, low whistle followed by, "Damn my eyes," brought her at a run. She barked her shin in her rush, and pain shot up her leg. The next corner brought her into a cave twice the size of the entry one. Breath caught in her throat, and her heart galloped into triple time.

Mages were laid out in rows, tied down with iron manacles at wrist and ankle. The shackles had been staked into the ground. She blanched at row upon row of trapped mages. There must be fifty of them, some moaning piteously, but most silently following the newly arrived mages and shifters with hooded eyes.

Jeremiah had joined the eleven others who arrived

before them. The cave wasn't cold, but shivers tracked down Renee's body until she started to shake. Before her teeth began chattering, she got hold of her horror, shoving it aside.

Niall, Sarai, and Stephan ran lightly to her. "Christ and all the damnable saints, but this is horrible," Niall said. "Worse than my worst-case imaginings."

"No way will we have enough power to transport them out of here," Stephan added.

"Not in one trip," Sarai agreed.

Jeremiah darted close, his face carved in grim lines. "Only one way to handle this."

Stephan nodded once. "Let's do it. Then we have to leave fast."

Renee wasn't following. "What exactly are we doing?"

"We can't move them," Sarai said in a voice quiet as death.

"So we have to summon mage fire and kill them here." Jeremiah gritted the words out.

Renee felt as if someone had punched her in the guts. "But they're shackled," she blurted. "If we burn them, their spirits will remain trapped." She stuffed a cork in the flow of words. Didn't add she was a healer, not a murderess. The others might not work at the business of saving lives, but none of them were in the habit of mowing down helpless victims, either.

Her soul rebelled at the task that lay ahead. Fifty magic wielders were a lot. It would put a huge dent in the mage population. She reminded herself how much she distrusted mages, but the argument didn't fly. Rather than feeling vindicated, she felt horrified and sick at heart.

"No choice," Jeremiah said in the same choked tone. "If we loose them, they'll turn on us. Anger is all that's left of them, and burning is the only way to free them from vampire control. They haven't been turned, but vamps have this entire lot in thrall exactly as we suspected."

"Aye, 'tis what's keeping them docile. Why they haven't tried to escape." Niall's brogue was as thick as it had been back in the Old Country, displaying his torment at their lack of options.

Renee gazed at Jeremiah. If this was tough for her, it must be killing him, yet he was moving forward. These were his people, never mind he was a shifter now. He was about to annihilate men he knew. Women too, she noted from a quick glance at the rows of bodies.

One caught her gaze. "Please," a woman with lank blonde hair pleaded. "I'm no harm to anyone. I was in the wrong place at the wrong time and ended up trapped. I have children." Bloodshot blue eyes flooded with tears.

Renee took a step toward her, but Jeremiah closed a hand around her arm, his fingers harsh as a vise. "No."

The word—and his grip—stopped her in her tracks.

"We rid the world of all of them. Now," he thundered. "We don't have the luxury of sorting if any are innocent."

Magic boiled around him, and the other mages ran to his side. Niall, Sarai, and Stephan wove their magic with his. After a pained pause while she watched the blonde mage weep and struggle against her manacles, Renee pitched her power into the group spell.

Fire rose in a sheet above them. Driven by magic, it raced the length of the cave and blanketed the lines of mages starting with those farthest away. Smoke and flames thickened the air, making breathing difficult. The charred stench of burning flesh twisted her stomach into a knot.

She swallowed back bile. What the fuck had happened to her toughness? She'd never been one to shy away from doing hard things.

Yeah, but this is worse than anything I've ever had to do by a factor of ten.

Renee switched to breathing through her mouth. She kept her magic flowing until Jeremiah shouted. "It's enough. Hurry." She stumbled back the way she'd come. Smoke shrouded the ley lines, and they glowed a sickly red behind its ashy coating.

Gasping and panting, she joined the group as all of them stumbled from the cave and onto a small patch of ground between its maw and the river. Black smoke rolled from the cave's entrance, along with the meaty smells of roasting flesh.

The bile she'd swallowed time and again erupted, and she bent to puke as her stomach emptied itself of a dinner she barely remembered eating. Above the stench of mage fire stripping flesh from bone, another smell intruded.

One she knew far too well.

"Vampires!" she shouted just as Jeremiah staggered from the cave.

"Leave," he cried. "We'll regroup in Golddust."

An image of the ghost town blasted into her head. Magic bubbled as mages and shifters beat a retreat. She waited, but Jeremiah's form didn't waver. She ran to him and gripped his arm. "Come on. We have to go too. They'll be here in seconds."

Her answer was a roar blasting from his throat. "I'm staying long enough to kill those fuckers. Because of them, I murdered my kinfolk." He turned on her, blue eyes blazing with hatred. "Do you understand? I murdered my kin. Mowed them down in cold blood. I demand revenge."

She wanted to tell him he was a courageous fool, that his bravery humbled her, but this was no place for emotion. Instead, she said, "Remaining is a death sentence, but I'll be damned if I leave you by yourself."

He shook out of her grasp. "Not your fight. Leave. Meet the others in Golddust. Tell them I'll be along presently."

"It is my fight. This touches every magic wielder."

Before she could launch more arguments, clothing shredded, falling around him in rough strips. The air glistened, hot and viscous with the unique aspect of Jeremiah's power—until the cave lion emerged. And then, power burned brighter still.

Damn. The beast was even bigger than she remembered.

She stood straight. Vampires were almost upon them, their characteristic rotten-meat stench dense and cloying. "I'm not leaving you," she announced and summoned shift magic. The eagle jumped to her call faster than she'd ever known it to.

Wings spread, she rose into the smoky air, shrieking a battle cry. How the hell they'd deal with vampires remained to be seen. No iron blades in sight, but it didn't seem to worry Jeremiah. With a shock, she realized she was coming to trust him.

A black portal edged with red flames formed

below. Vampires surged through. Six of them. Not bad. She'd dealt with four, and she wasn't alone anymore.

"How dare you? Those mages were ours. Ours!" The vamp in the lead shook a fist at the cave lion. Robes of dark-green silk billowed around him. Black hair shot with silver fell to waist level, and his handsome face was screwed into a furious expression. Silver eyes rimmed with red narrowed to slits, and power blazed from his hands in mini lightning bolts.

So far, the vamps were focused on the lion. Did they even see her? If they did, did they realize she was more than just one more eagle on the hunt for prey?

Renee kicked herself. If this morning hadn't happened, she might pull off her "one more eagle" ploy, but they had the feel of her, the scent of her. These weren't the same batch as this morning, but they had ways of communicating. Once they noticed her, they'd pull a similar stunt and force her out of the sky.

She couldn't afford to let that happen, and she hastily constructed an invisibility spell. They were hit-or-miss affairs when she was in bird form. It was damned near impossible to shroud every part of herself because flight was a dynamic process, and she was always on the move. Best she could hope for was to construct a 3D rectangle and remain within it.

The lion roared and roared again before it surged forward, aiming for the fist-shaking vampire.

Understanding full well it was under attack, the vampire turned the full force of his gaze on the lion, chanting in a singsong voice.

Renee had been watching so closely, she overflew her protective spell and pulled a wingtip back to where it couldn't be seen. She'd heard about vampire mind control but hadn't seen it in action. The crew this morning had been toying with her. If they'd been serious about hypnotizing her, the outcome might have been far different.

Would the vamp chanting below nab her too?

Did the fact she and Jeremiah were together—like it said in the lore books—confer any added protection at all?

"Yes," the eagle answered her unspoken question, and then added, *"The coercion spell isn't aimed at us. Not yet, but we must be ready."*

Interesting. The spells were target-specific. What would that mean for Jeremiah? Would he be strong enough to resist?

Seemingly oblivious to the vampire's spell, the lion took a running leap and launched itself at the vampire. Closing its jaws around the abomination's neck, it bit clean through. Two more chomps, and the vampire's head rolled in the dust. Blood sprayed, coating the lion with black and red ichor. It shook free of the vampire and leapt on the next nearest one, repeating its actions.

The beast was so large, the vampire's neck fit easily within its mouth. This vamp only took two bites to dispatch. Renee wanted to cheer. She also wanted to help, but the lion was doing fine without her.

The other four vampires, two with black hair, one blond, and one russet-haired one screamed their ire. Their voices were harsh, like rusty metal grating against itself, and they spoke a language she'd never heard. They rushed the lion, two from each side, and glommed onto its flanks and neck with their fangs.

The lion roared loud enough to shake the earth, but it couldn't dislodge the vampires. It rolled, but the vamps still didn't let go. Horror shot through her. She'd thought the lion invincible, but something was wrong.

She had to help.

"*Time to fight.*" The eagle's words solidified her resolve.

She flew from her hiding place straight for the nearest vampire. It was sluggish, lost in a feeding haze, so it didn't notice her until she drove her beak into one eye. It let go of the lion long enough to shriek. She pivoted and put out his other eye. The vamp would recover, but not anytime soon.

Meanwhile, he was blind. It had to slow him down.

Renee wheeled away from his hands pawing the air as he tried to catch her. The next vampire was just as lost in bloodlust as his buddy had been. The blind one screeched something she assumed was a warning, but she didn't hesitate. Her beak drove straight and true, right through the next vampire's eye and on into whatever it had for brains.

It regrouped faster than the first one and closed a hand over her body. Undeterred, she took advantage of him holding onto her and jammed her beak into his other eye. He tightened his hold, intent on destroying her. Desperate to escape, she pecked his face, hitting every nerve she could think of. When she plunged her beak into his ear, he let go, shrieking in agony.

If she'd been human, she'd have laughed. Nothing like decimating an eardrum to create red-hot agony. She flapped higher into the air, beyond reach of the other two. The ones who could still see.

They were still latched onto the lion, but with only two to deal with, the beast lurched upright and headed right into the river flowing at flood stage. The blind vamps still squealed with pain, but they shambled after the lion. Because they couldn't see, the current caught them, hurtling them downstream. One's robes caught on a snag sticking into the river. For a heart-stopping moment, she was afraid it would save him, but the branch snapped under his weight, and he raced after the other vampire, straight for the falls.

Four down. Two to go.

The lion swam against the current, holding its

position in a spot that forced both vampires against sharp rocks. The lion had far more mass than both vamps together, and it held them underwater where the roiling cascade pounded their bodies into lethal rocks.

Renee flew in tight circles overhead, cawing. Vampires didn't need to breathe, but their flesh was being shredded against the rocks. Surely, they'd let go. The water above them turned sludgy, filled with red and black streamers from their disintegrating bodies. At least the fast rushing water cut their stench a little.

First one and then the other swept by her, carried downstream by the vicious current. She waited, expecting the lion to lumber out of the water, but it just stood there.

"*What's wrong?*" she shouted.

It didn't answer. Neither did Jeremiah.

"*Come on,*" she urged. "*We have to leave.*" She didn't bother adding more vamps would show up. They were like a cancer, malignant and ubiquitous.

With her worry escalating to panic, Renee gathered magic into a travel spell. Draping it around all of them, she unleashed her casting, holding an image of Golddust front and center. "*Hang on,*" she told Jeremiah. "*Once we're out of here, I'll figure out what's going on and fix it.*"

Her spell was lethargic, slow to take hold, but they

weren't going all that far. She directed her power, pulling it back when it slopped over the edges. Just when she was starting to fear she'd made a mistake, picked the wrong location, the black surrounding them developed a grayish tint.

"It's okay. We're almost there." She used her best soothing voice, the one she employed for sick patients.

A weak snarl yielded to Jeremiah's voice. *"Where?"*

"Golddust. Where else?"

"Aw shit. I have to shift."

Anger simmered, displacing compassion. *"You will do no such thing until I determine what those bastards did to you. Christ on a cracker, are you still ashamed of being a shifter?"*

The lion roared louder.

Good, she thought. Nothing like a proud bondmate to whip a shifter into shape.

"Never was ashamed." His voice was thin, broken. *"Hard day for my people. Seeing me like this will be one more shock."*

She took a breath and blew it out, clacking her beak. *"Don't you get it, yet? From now on, we're the same people. No more mine and yours. Have faith. The mages in Golddust will rally behind you once they know what you did. The shifters sure as hell will."*

She brought them out on Golddust's rocky main street just as dawn was breaking. The lion was on his feet. Barely. His head hung low, and his breathing was labored. Everyone ran to them, forming a tight circle. Renee summoned shift magic. She needed her human form to assess Jeremiah's injuries. Cold from the sub-freezing morning attacked her nakedness. She ignored it.

Please. Let it only be blood loss, she prayed and directed magic into scanning the lion. Why was it so listless? Bond animals never got sick.

"Who's with you?" Johnny asked, dark eyes wide with wonder.

Chloe strode forward. "It's Jeremiah. My brother. He's hurt, but Renee brought him back to us." Chloe wrapped her arms as far around the cave lion's neck as she could and buried her face in its ruff. The beast mewled as if it was in terrible pain and pitched onto its side in the dirt with Chloe on top of it.

Niall joined Renee, sending his own magic cascading through the lion. He cursed in Gaelic, but she'd already figured it out. "How could this be?" she screamed.

"Ye ran afoul of master vampires," Niall said. "Their poison is eroding the lion's magic, its link to the animals' special world."

Chloe raised a tearstained face. "You have to save Jeremiah. And his lion."

"Give us room to work." Renee didn't recognize the

grim voice as hers. Nor did she bother to inform Chloe that her brother's fate was inextricably linked with the lion's. Power flared as Niall shared his magical center with her.

"Take what ye need," he said gruffly.

"Thanks." Honing power into a laser-sharp blade, she carved a series of slashes through the lion's thick hide. She tasted blood from biting through her lower lip but kept right on slicing incisions. At first nothing happened, but then a viscous black fluid oozed from the slits. It stank of vampire.

"Good job," Niall said. "I'll do the next set."

She was panting from effort, no longer cold despite her nakedness. "Cut here." She pointed.

"Aye." Niall repeated her actions. "And here as well?"

"Yes." Once these drain, we'll assess what we have."

Voices rose and fell around her, but she didn't care what the mages thought. If any of them said one negative word about Jeremiah or his cave lion, she'd rip them to shreds.

arlier at the Cave:

Jeremiah funneled as much power as he could to his bondmate. Something had happened to the lion when the vampires were feeding from it. Something bad, but he wasn't sure what it was or how to fix it. They'd defeated the vamps with Renee's help, but now the lion stood in the river, not moving. It was wedged between boulders, but its grip on the rock-littered bottom wasn't all that strong. Jeremiah was afraid they'd be swept over the falls if the beast didn't lumber out of the fast-running torrent.

He tried to shift, so he could move them back onto dry ground, but his attempt was laughable. Things grew hazy after that, maybe because his magic was down to bedrock, but Renee got them out of there somehow. He came back to himself, kind of, when they were close to Golddust. He still wanted to shift, but she dressed him down.

Maybe she was right, but this wasn't the way he wanted his kinsmen to find out about the lion. He wanted them to accept his new status, not be horrified by it.

Hell, he probably didn't have enough magic left to shift anyway.

Renee was amazing. He tried to tell her but couldn't get a grasp on enough of anything to power telepathy. She was brave, resourceful. She'd stuck by him after he told her to leave. And she'd saved him. He wasn't under any illusions. Without her aid, he and the lion would still be in the river—or pitched up on rocks at the bottom of the falls. More vampires would show up. Once it happened, he'd be dead—or worse, turned. The lion could return to the animals' world...

Maybe not. If it could leave, why hadn't it? He tried to ask, but the beast didn't answer.

Something wasn't right. His thoughts were all over the map, his normally incisive mental ability absent. Maybe he needed to be back in his own body, but he didn't have enough magic left to light a match, let alone shift. The lion was...different. It had moved from an active entity sharing his consciousness to an inert lump.

Did bond animals do that?

He wished he knew more, but it was like wishing for... For what? He couldn't think. Consciousness was elusive. Remaining awake was important, though he wasn't certain how he knew that. Yet if he didn't stay on top of it, he felt himself slipping down a long, meandering tunnel. Lights flickered, welcoming lights. He wanted to reach for them, go to them, but then he dragged himself back.

The lion fell over with a thud that rattled him. What was happening?

Stay centered. Stay focused.

But he was tired, so tired. Pain lanced across his ribs. He struggled weakly but was trapped in the lion's body. Its pain was his pain. No escape. More cuts followed until he lost count.

He screamed, the sound absorbed by the lion's presence.

Pressure built until whatever was left of him had to crack wide open. Agony seared him. How could he hurt this much without a body? He curled the body he didn't have into a ball, determined not to cry out again.

"Sorry. I'm sorry." The lion's words were a breathy whisper, but it was the first the beast had spoken since the vampire attack.

Jeremiah hunted for something to say, but words slipped away, lost in a haze of knives and needles scoring his flesh. At least hanging onto consciousness had moved to a distant back burner. Pain was everything. Throbbing, jabbing, burning, excruciating. His vision hazed, first red then black and gray.

Reality smacked him hard. No one could hurt this much and still live.

I can't give up. I can't.

He inhaled a jagged breath, edged with what felt like glass shards scoring throat and lungs. Blowing it out, he did it again. The universe narrowed to each breath. As long as he was still breathing, he wasn't dead.

If it wouldn't have sent his pain through the ceiling, he'd have laughed. The harsh, bitter bursts would have damn near done him in. Time passed—a little or a lot. Impossible to tell.

Finally, a breath wasn't quite as painful. He thought he was imagining it, that something critical had finally broken beyond redemption, and he was losing ground to the battle raging through the lion's body.

The next breath was easier still. He latched onto a slender thread of hope. When he reached for his magic to shape telepathy, it didn't exactly leap to his command, but it was there.

"*Sorry for what?*" he croaked, remembering the lion's apology.

"*Vampires. I forgot.*"

"Forgot what?" Jeremiah was confused.

The beast panted, breath sounds rough as it fought to communicate. *"Master vampires, old ones, carry venom."* A bevy of pants drowned out its next words.

Jeremiah breathed deeper, his first almost-pain-free breath in what felt like forever. *"Vamps don't need poison. They mesmerize their prey."*

"Different," the lion rasped. *"That's mental coercion. This is an actual toxin, but only for magic-wielders."*

"But why?"

A muted whuffling roar heartened Jeremiah. The lion was recovering. *"We hunted them. They needed a way to immobilize us."*

Jeremiah's mind was returning to his control rather than scattering unrelated bits of data willy-nilly. He culled through memories of vampires, but he'd always given them a wide berth.

"Most of this happened prior to your birth," the lion inserted.

"Jer?" Chloe's telepathy cut through the mush his thoughts had been. *"Please try. We're all rooting for you."*

"I'll be okay." He aimed for reassuring, but his words were strained.

"He heard me. He heard me!" Chloe shrieked from somewhere close by. "Renee. He finally heard me."

"Excellent news." Relief thrummed beneath Renee's words. "Hang on. I'm not quite done."

Jeremiah would have grinned if he could. He'd rejoined the world outside the lion's body. *"It's all right,"* he reassured the lion. *"I don't blame you for anything. We won. We killed them, and we'll live to fight another day."*

"Spoken like a true warrior. I'm proud to call you bondmate."

Gratitude surged. They'd moved past their initial feinting around each other. The lion may have chosen him, but neither had been sure of the other until their bond was tested.

Between burning mages and the vampire confrontation, they'd solidified their connection, forged it into an unbreakable pledge.

"Renee?" If Chloe could hear him, it boded well for telepathy getting through.

"Yup. You are one stubborn bastard, but you're going to pull through." She didn't bother with telepathy. No need. He heard her loud and clear.

The words were so typically Renee, he wanted to pull her into his arms and never let go. Kiss her until she melted against him. He settled for, *"Thank you. You saved my life. And my bondmate too."* Encouraged he summoned power, intent on shifting.

"Nooooo," she screeched. "No shifting until I'm

done. What began on one form must be completed on the same form. If you shift now, goddess only knows what the result will be. I haven't worked this hard, expended gobs of magic only to—"

"*It's all right,*" he cut in. "*Tell me when you're ready.*"

"You're not going to argue with me?" Incredulity underscored her words.

"Appears he has more sense than you give him credit for." Niall's brogue was welcome. Jeremiah wanted to hug him too. And Chloe and Stephan and every single mage.

He projected his consciousness beyond the lion lying on its side. They were in Golddust, but he'd known that part. His housemates sat in a circle around the lion. Stephan, Sarai, Niall, and Renee were bent over him, feeding magic into long cuts scoring the lion's rib cage, rump, and chest.

He remembered when the eagle shifter had healed him. Different poison, same strategy. Provide exit points and lure the poison out.

"*Will we need to roll over?*" he asked.

"Think I liked it better when you were comatose," Renee mumbled.

"He's only trying to help." Defensiveness ran hot beneath Chloe's words.

"Sorry. I know. I'm tired, but that's not a good excuse." Renee exhaled in a whoosh.

Flashes of heat scored him where she closed the wounded places, sealing them with magic.

The lion purred and scrambled upright, swaying slightly on its feet.

"Hang on," Renee cautioned. "I need to check the side that was in the dirt." She ran her hands over the lion, dusting debris from its tawny coat. The lion purred louder, and the corners of Renee's mouth twitched into something that looked suspiciously like a smile.

Jeremiah wished he was human, that her warm touch was traversing his flesh, not the lion's fur. If he'd had a cock, it would have stirred, but the lion seemed impervious to sexual imagery. Good thing. He didn't want to embarrass himself.

"*We're good,*" the lion informed him. "*A bit of residual toxin, but nothing I can't clear on my own.*"

Jeremiah waited for Renee's permission. She'd risked herself when she didn't have to. He'd told her to leave, but she'd remained by his side. Ceding control over when he shifted to her judgement was a small concession.

One he was more than willing to make.

"*What are you waiting for?*" the lion pressed. "*I*

would return to the animals' world where I can complete my healing."

"Renee. I'm waiting for her."

"I heard that." Her tone was dry, but this time understated humor laced into her words. "Go ahead, shifter. Find your human form. I've done all I can. By the goddess's grace, it was enough."

He opened himself, letting the unfamiliar shift magic run through him. Bones reformed, skin reshaped itself. Fur fell away, replaced by the familiar planes of his body.

A roar blasted from his mouth, followed by a deep purr rumbling through his chest. *"I shall return presently,"* the lion informed him.

Jeremiah turned in a circle, gazing at men and women he'd known for centuries, staring at him gape-mouthed.

Chloe moved to his side and wrapped an arm around his shoulders. "Does anyone have a jacket to spare?"

Johnny, Raul, and Liam shrugged out of theirs, offering them.

"I only need one," Jeremiah said, moved by their generosity. "I'll take Raul's. It's longest." He shrugged into it, grateful for its fur-lined warmth. A quick glance at the sky showed the sun skirting the western horizon. It had been dawn when they'd arrived.

Realization carved a path through him. "We were here all day?"

Chloe nodded. "The healing took a long time."

"Aye, mate," Niall spoke up. "'Tis worried I was we were too late, that the poison had too great a toehold to defeat."

"Had it been any bondmate other than your lion," Sarai cut in, "we might not have been so fortunate."

"Your beast is strong," Renee said from where she'd sunk to a squat in the center of the circle. "Still, it was indeed nip and tuck." An oversized gray-flannel shirt covered her, no doubt borrowed since she'd have been naked after she shifted. Her legs, long and shapely, were bent beneath her, and her bare feet streaked with dirt.

Jeremiah bent and offered her a hand. She took it and let him draw her upright. Lines of strain carved deep into her forehead and inscribed pinwheels at the outer edges of her eyes. If he assessed her with his own power, he'd find hers had run perilously low.

Still holding her hand, he bowed to her. When he straightened, he said, "I owe you my life. Words are inadequate, but you have my undying thanks."

She shrugged, and color rose, dotting her cheeks. "I'm a healer. It's what I do."

"Bullshit," Niall said succinctly. "I've never seen anyone work harder, draw deeper from themselves than you did today. My hat is off to you, Madam Healer. You refused to acknowledge defeat."

"Even when it stared you in the face," Stephan muttered. "I was here too. I felt death's presence."

Renee turned a deeper shade of rose. "I don't like to lose." She tugged her hand out of Jeremiah's, leaving an empty spot he yearned to fill, and went to stand next to Niall and Sarai.

Johnny approached Jeremiah. "When were you going to tell us about your, uh, new magic?" The mage shook black hair over his shoulders.

"It's a fair question," Jeremiah agreed. "This transformation is brand new—"

"I told them that," Chloe butted in. "I told them everything. How you thought it would be best to wait until after we visited Mitch's stronghold, so as not to muddy the waters. How you—"

"Whoa." Jeremiah held up a hand.

"It was all right," Johnny said. "Chloe loves you. She wasn't trying to steal your thunder."

"You weren't here to speak for yourself," Raul pointed out.

"I'm not angry," Jeremiah said, pleased the mages were defending his sister "Do any of you have questions? I wasn't trying to pull something sneaky or hide my bondmate. In truth, I was still getting used to the idea of being a shifter. It's a pretty big leap after being a mage for centuries and growing up steeped in hatred for the other side of our magical circle."

There it was. He'd tossed the issue of their mutual ambivalence out on the table. More than ambivalence. They'd been at war with their shifter cousins. It was one of the things that had driven all of them from the Old Country. The never-ending hostilities—along with rabid clerics out for their blood. America was a bigger place than the U.K. or even Europe. More room to spread out.

"I'll admit I was plenty pissed when Chloe told us," Raul spoke slowly. "But I've had all day to get past it." He grinned crookedly. "If you scratch the surface and are honest, not a mage standing hasn't wished for a bond animal at one time or another."

"I believe things may be changing," Sarai said.

"What do you mean?" Niall asked.

"My psychic pursuits don't yield precise answers, but we're at the tail end of all twelve of the major astrological ages, an epoch that takes almost thirty thousand years from start to finish. Significant changes are afoot as we embark on the next cycle. One may have to do with the schism between mages and shifters. It only showed up at the tail end of the current cycle, and it appears to be repairing itself."

"My lion said much the same thing," Jeremiah murmured.

"As did my eagle," Renee added.

"Excellent news," Johnny said. "I'm old enough to barely recall when we were one people."

Jeremiah angled his head to one side. "Do you remember why some of us picked the mage path and others a shifter one?"

"Not with any level of precision. Naturally, mages who'd already bonded retained their mates. The new generation of magic wielders that came along around the time of the Crusades were different. Some bonded. Others never found an animal to link with. Over time, we evolved into mages and shifters. Rather than hanging onto our common magical roots, we became mired in distrust for one another."

He stopped to take a measured breath. "On my side, I was one of those who never bonded. I recall being frustrated and angry, feeling cheated out of what should have been my birthright. It wasn't a quantum leap from there to signing on with disgruntled mages who lost sight of our commonalities and homed in on our differences instead."

"Maybe if we put energy toward repairing the breach, we can hasten healing and ensure we never have a repeat of today." Jeremiah swallowed around a tight place in his throat.

"Today was pretty horrible." Chloe grimaced. "I talked tough about killing the other mages, but the only way I got through it was by not thinking and powering forward."

"It's the only way any of us got through it, lass," Niall muttered.

Jeremiah unclenched his jaw. "Other than Mitch's relatives, did you recognize anyone?" He'd been so thunderstruck by the sheer numbers of shackled mages, he hadn't taken the time to inspect them. To put a finer point on it, he'd been afraid if he identified too many, he wouldn't have been able to call mage fire to kill them.

He gazed at the mages, seeing sad, slow nods all around the circle. His heart ached for his friends. "I'm not sure this will help, but even if we had another shot at today, I'd make the same decision. Not that evil can't be salvaged, but we barely escaped the vampires as things stood."

"They'll still be a problem." Johnny spoke flatly.

"Maybe not. We wiped out the magic that was strengthening them," Chloe said.

"Nah." Stephan walked closer. "They've had a taste of freedom. They'll not retreat to their nasty shadows easily. Beyond that, we've pissed the crap out of them. They'll be out for blood." He skewered Jeremiah with his unremitting gaze. "How many did you kill today—after the rest of us left?"

"Six vamps showed up. Only two of them are dead

for certain. The others are injured, courtesy of Renee's beak and an impromptu trip down the river, but they can recover from most anything."

Stephan raked his hands through his blond hair. "You can bet they won't rest until they avenge your attack. Sarai and I were among the first to be captured as they experimented with their enhanced power. And Marie."

Jeremiah bowed his head. "I am so sorry for the loss of your mate."

Shadows flitted across Stephan's face. "I vowed when I lost her, I wouldn't rest until the last vampires were defanged—or ran from this country knowing if they stayed, it would spell their doom."

"What happens next?" Renee asked, so weary she swayed on her feet.

"We go home and get some rest," Jeremiah said.

"Good plan, but where?" Sarai countered. "After today, the vamps have all our scents. I hope I'm wrong, but I'd be surprised if they didn't launch an attack. And sooner, rather than later."

"Our house is big enough to accommodate four more," Chloe said. "How about where you live?"

"Fourteen would be tight," Stephan said. "I'd prefer to return to my home, but the prudent course is for us to join you."

Jeremiah pressed his lips together to hide the smile

that wanted out. Renee would be under the same roof with him. He could test the waters with her. Thank her again. Tell her how much he admired her. How beautiful she was. How brave. How much he wanted to protect her for the rest of their lives.

What a fucking coward I am. What I need to tell her is I'm falling in love with her.

A quick glance in her direction convinced him she needed sleep far more than a mistimed declaration of love. They were fighting on the same side, and they felt a whole lot more like allies than they had twenty-four hours before, but nothing else had changed.

She still didn't like him. Yeah, she'd gone all out to save him, but it was the cave lion she'd been attending to. One of the most ancient bond animals. Of course, she'd do everything in her power to ensure its survival. His was ancillary.

He squared his shoulders. Weariness dogged him too. Nothing like engaging in genocide for a generation's worth of mages, almost dying himself, and living through intransigent pain to sap a man.

"Ready to leave?" Chloe asked from where she stood next to him.

"Yeah. Ready to fall on my face is more like it."

"We'll meet at your place," Niall called.

"Be there soon," Sarai added.

Jeremiah didn't like the sound of that. He leveled

his gaze at the four shifters. "You're going home first, aren't you?"

Stephan nodded. "Yes, but only long enough to grab clean clothes."

"We'll be in and out of there fast," Sarai said. She tried to smile, but it didn't quite happen.

"Bad idea," Jeremiah retorted. "What if vamps are there? They wouldn't even have to track you. They know where you live. It's where they nabbed you the day they killed Marie."

Stephan squeezed his eyes shut, and Jeremiah chided himself for being so blunt, but these were harsh times. No latitude to sugarcoat anything. Not really. Before he could stumble through an apology, Stephan rolled his shoulders back.

"You're right, of course. None of us are thinking all that clearly right now."

"And nowhere is safe," Renee mumbled. "It's the hardest part for me to wrap my head around. I keep thinking it's a normal world and business as usual because I want it to be true."

His heart cracked open; the need to shelter her from harm ran fierce. It took all his self-control not to go to her, gather her close.

"Come on." Chloe clapped her hands together. "There's a pot of soup on the back of the stove and fresh bread. We'll all do better with a spot of food—and a few hours of shut-eye."

Jeremiah waited until magic boiled around the group, turning the air vivid with colors. Once he was convinced everyone was headed for their rambling Victorian in Silverthorne, he called magic of his own and set a travel spell to take him home.

Renee would be there. Even if she didn't want him, just being in proximity to her made him feel whole. He'd take his victories as he could get them. They made the wasteland today had been easier to stomach.

CHAPTER 10

Renee barely remembered eating. Or dressing. One of the female mages had loaned her a pair of jeans, a long-sleeved T-shirt, and underwear. Someone had scrounged a pair of sandals that almost fit, along with thick woolen socks. Once they were done eating, Chloe had led the way upstairs, opened a door, and showed her where bed linens and towels were, but making the bed felt quite beyond her. She'd pitched onto a double bed in a room on the third floor, not bothering to remove her borrowed garments beyond the shoes. Once she was prone, she rolled herself into a quilt and called it even.

She woke with a start, staring into the dark. Where was she? And then she remembered. They were all at Jeremiah's house. It had been on the early side when she'd passed out, and now it was deep night. Maybe two or three in the morning. She unwound the quilt and found her way to a nearby bathroom, splashing cold water on her face once she got there. She'd never undressed, and she padded downstairs to the kitchen, intent on finding more to eat.

She still felt hollow inside, as if there wasn't enough food or rest in the world to wipe out the day she'd lived through.

"Throw yourself a pity party, why don't you?" she mumbled as she wandered into the kitchen, her stocking-clad feet cold on the hardwood floor. They'd finished the homemade soup, but a quick riffle through the pantry turned up a can of chili. She dragged a can opener off the wall and transferred the contents to a small saucepan.

While it heated on the stove, she cracked a beer, savoring the bite as it traveled down her throat. Deciding lukewarm was good enough, she turned off the flame beneath her pot and moved to the table, placing the small saucepan on a towel. She'd polished most of it off when footsteps caught her attention.

Damn. She hoped she'd been quiet and hadn't wakened anyone.

Jeremiah walked into the kitchen, stopping shy of the table. He was wrapped in a threadbare white terry cloth robe that clung to his broad shoulders, highlighting muscles and the elegant lines of his body.

He offered a perfunctory nod before looking away. "I'm sorry. Didn't mean to disturb your meal."

"You didn't. I'm nearly done, or I'd offer to share it with you." She grinned. "There's more chili. I'm a whiz with a can opener. Want me to heat some for you?" Renee picked up the beer and drank deeply. She'd treated him almost like a friend. Probably a bad approach since he didn't like her much. He was plenty grateful she'd saved his bondmate—and him—but it wasn't the same as appreciating her for herself.

Not by a long shot.

She drained the bottle and wished for whiskey as silence stretched between them. It was his house, and if he didn't want her cluttering up his kitchen, he could tell her to go back upstairs once she was done eating. In fact, she'd save him the trouble. Two more bites and she'd be gone, except her appetite had fled. He was so close—and so masculine—she was having a hard time breathing.

"Sure, Renee. That would be nice," he said.

She'd been so deep in crafting her escape route, it took her a moment to remember her offer to heat food for him.

He cracked the fridge and extracted two more beers, handing her one. "Looks like you could use a refill."

"Thanks." She twisted the top off. "Although I was considering something harder."

"We have whiskey. I can grab some from the liquor cabinet. Did you get any sleep?"

"Oh yeah. I passed out. First I've stirred since your sister showed me my room."

"Good. You deserve a whole lot more than a bit of rest. You were a real hero today." He ducked into the pantry and returned brandishing a can of beef stew. "Back in a flash with something more alcoholic than beer."

She got to her feet, rinsed out her chili pan, and filled it with canned stew, turning the flame to medium. As soon as he got back, she'd pour herself a jot of booze and retreat to her room. No reason for both of them to be uncomfortable.

Renee winced. Who knew how he was feeling, but if she remained, she'd have a hell of a hard time keeping her hands off his body. The bathrobe displayed enough of his chest to fascinate her. Not that she hadn't seen him naked when he shifted, but she'd been in healer mode then.

Not anymore. Now she was painfully aware of his body—and hers. Of breasts with nipples that were already hard. Of labia swollen and slick with need. Arousal ran hot, and all he'd done was ask if she'd gotten a decent few hours of rest.

Christ, she was pathetic.

Worse, something was wrong with her. She'd been around attractive men before—lots of them. What was it about this one that drew her as if he were a male version of a Siren perched on a rock churning out irresistible music? It couldn't be the prophecy she'd plucked from the lore book. They were never this precise, relying on metaphor rather than specifics.

If not that, then what?

Jeremiah walked back into the kitchen, an amber bottle tucked beneath one arm and two tumblers in hand. He plunked the tumblers on the table and drew the bottle out. "All I could find was home brew, but Raul's wife creates a mean mix. You might want to dilute it with water. I bet it's 150-proof."

The smell of stew on the edge of burning drove her to the stove. She yanked the pot off the burner, stirring madly. "Sorry. I'm sorry." She turned the flame off and moved the hot pan above a tile counter. "Caught it before it scorched. At least not too badly."

"Put the pan down and come over here."

Something in his voice made her apprehensive and drew her at the same time. Was this when he shoved a tumbler of whiskey into her hand and sent her upstairs? Despite her resolve to grab the booze and run, she was loathe to leave his presence.

She set the pan on a trivet and made her way to the

table. "I truly am sorry. The stew's still edible. I caught it before it was ruined. And if you don't want it, I can start fresh with another can." She was babbling, but she couldn't make herself shut up.

In a fast, fluid move, he scooted in front of her and dropped his hands onto her shoulders. "Look at me. Please."

"It's okay," she mumbled. "I'll just get some of that home brew and leave you to your meal."

"Look at me," he repeated, not moving his hands off her shoulders.

Warmth from his touch seared her, making her other problem—the one of wanting to touch him so badly she could taste it—far more pressing. Her swollen labia rubbed against one another, and she swallowed a low groan. She had to get out of here to somewhere she could jam her hand between her legs and bring herself off. Just touching herself would do it. She was that close and didn't understand how her arousal had gone from low key to a hundred percent in such a short time.

To hurry her exit along, she raised her gaze to meet his. Twin flames burned in the depths of his blue eyes, and a soft smile turned his mouth into something profanely beautiful. "Better. I will never hurt you."

"Didn't think you would," she mumbled. "I should leave."

He tightened his grip. "What if I don't want you to? What if I told you I sensed you here and came into the kitchen on purpose to intercept you?"

Surprise raced through her. "Why would you do that?"

He moved one hand to cup the side of her face. She tried not to, but leaned into his touch, craving more of it. Of him.

"We got off to a rocky start, you and I," he went on, his deep voice like a balm. "But I have a confession to make."

"You don't have to thank me again," she murmured. "Truly you don't."

He shook his head. "That's not it. When you arrived at Stephan's, I was inside, and I spent a really long time peeking through the window at you." He took a deep breath, but his gaze never left her face. "I was fascinated, entranced. You're so lovely, what man wouldn't be? But you're not just stunning to look at. You're brave, selfless, capable. I know I was a mage, and you don't trust us, but—"

"It was wrong of me," she cut in, anxious to correct his misperception. "I'm over it. Our magic is the same. Not better or worse. Hell, not even different."

A corner of his mouth twisted downward, and he cradled the side of her head, lacing his fingers into her uncombed curls. "I'm walking around what I want to say."

She leaned closer, near enough their bodies were almost touching. Heat from him eddied between them, and his scent—the one that had snared her earlier—returned with full force. Vanilla, rosemary, and freshly wet forest surrounded her, thick enough to eat.

"Maybe we don't need words," she murmured, suddenly shy but unable to look away from his amazing eyes. Up close like this, silvery flecks floated around the irises, making them shine.

"Perhaps not, but if you don't leave, I'm going to kiss you. I didn't come in here for food or drink. I came here for you."

Excitement shot from the soles of her feet up over the top of her head. He wanted her. Nothing shy of a tsunami could have dragged her from the kitchen, and maybe not even that. She turned her mouth upward, and he covered it with his. His chiseled lips felt just as enticing as she'd imagined they would. The first kiss was gentle. Too gentle.

She wrapped her arms around him and pressed her body the full length of his. He'd feel her pebbled nipples, but the time to be ashamed of her arousal was past. The length of him, hard, hot, and thick, pressed into her belly, and the evidence of his hunger thrilled her. She wanted to reach between them, wrap her hands around his cock, followed by her mouth. Imagining how his girth would stretch her fed her excitement, not that it needed encouragement.

He upped the ante on their kiss, which had turned more urgent and demanding. She opened her mouth to his questing tongue and sparred with it. He tasted sweet and hot, and she couldn't get enough of his mouth. They traded bites, kisses, and suckles. She bit and sealed each spot with kisses before biting again. He teased her mouth with his tongue, driving it inside and then withdrawing in a simulation of sex that stoked her lust.

He made a decidedly male sound and thrust his erection into her belly. Heat and need roared through her, and she straddled one of his legs, pressing her engorged nub against the firm muscles of his thigh. He grasped her ass and jammed his leg firmly between hers.

She writhed against him, desperate for contact, for release. If his mouth hadn't been glued against hers, she would have screamed as a climax shot through her, spun her around, and spat her out.

He ripped his mouth from hers, scooped an arm beneath her knees, and carried her out of the kitchen and down the darkened hallway to a staircase she wasn't familiar with. Narrow and winding, it led upward. She twined her arms around his neck, hanging on.

"I can walk," she managed, her breathing still running triple time.

"Not a chance. I'm not letting you get away."

She giggled. "What makes you think I'm about to make a run for it?"

"You. You said you were leaving multiple times, even after I returned with the liquor. Damn!"

"What?"

"I left the bottle downstairs, but I can run back for it."

Another very uncharacteristic giggle bubbled from her throat. "You just said it was risky to leave me alone."

He laughed too. "We'll be in my bedroom soon. I can seal it with magic. Wouldn't hold you long, but long enough for a quick trip downstairs."

She searched for a way to tell him he didn't need magic to bind her, but everything she came up with made her sound like a sex-starved slut. Hell, she'd already come, and he hadn't even touched her yet. "I don't need whiskey," she murmured. "Just you."

They crested the stairs, and he turned for the far end of the hall. "That's the most welcome thing I've heard in a long time." The last door on the right popped open, no doubt encouraged by a magical assist, and he carried her into a generous room tucked beneath the eaves. Dormer windows housed a padded seat with an armoire next to it. A large desk of polished wood graced one corner, and an old-fashioned bed another. The bed had high, carved head and footboards that appeared to be made of the same wood as the desk.

Candles in sconces flickered to life, casting the room in a warm, golden glow. Bookshelves overflowing with volumes, scrolls, and notebooks covered every vacant wall. The room felt like him. Solid. Masculine. No frills, but comfortable just the same.

He did set her on her feet then. Behind them, the door closed on its own. Jeremiah moved until he faced her then tucked an errant curl behind her ear. Offering a shy smile, he said, "I'm afraid I'm woefully out of practice, but you haven't run screaming from my room, so I'm assuming you want to be here."

She nodded. "I've never wanted anything quite so much." Hooking her hands beneath her T-shirt, she yanked it over her head. The sports bra she'd borrowed barely contained her breasts, and they spilled out on both sides.

A strangled groan burst from him, and he pushed the flimsy bra aside, filling his hands with her breasts. His touch was exquisite as he tweaked her erect nipples. Sensation shot from her breasts straight to her crotch, and it was as if she hadn't just come. She wanted more. Needed more.

A whole lot more.

Reaching between them, she jerked the sash of his robe, untying it. Once it was free, she pushed it off his shoulders where it pooled on the floor. He'd bent his head and was suckling her nipples, moving from one to the next. She sandwiched her hands between them and wrapped her fingers around his cock.

Hard. Hot. So ready, it quivered beneath her touch. She stroked him, holding him between her hands, and he groaned again. Straightening, he propelled her toward the bed. The covers were already down, and he lifted her onto a silky sheet. Hands at her waist, he undid the fastenings of her pants and pulled them down her legs, followed by her underwear.

He kicked them aside and stood over her, looking at her with an intensity that fed her soul. "You are so goddamned gorgeous." His words held a raspy edge. "I could look at you forever."

She took him in too, really looked at him. Muscles slabbed and bunched down arms and legs. His stomach was defined, and the cock she wanted to get to know a whole lot better rose from a spiky mat of golden curls. "You're the gorgeous one." She patted the bed in invitation.

He grinned, slow, lazy, wanton. Grabbing one of

her ankles with each hand, he spread her legs and knelt in front of her. After long moments where she willed him to do more than worship her with his eyes, he bent his head and strung kisses down her stomach. Her skin shivered beneath his tongue. He got close to her nub but then moved away.

Her body writhed, moving from side to side as her hips thrashed. She was desperate for the feel of him and more than ready when he slipped his hands beneath her, cupping her ass. Finally, after what felt like forever, he settled his mouth above her throbbing, aching clit, breathing on her. She bucked, frantic for contact, but he held her an angstrom away.

"Tell me," he urged. "Talk with me, darling."

"You know what I want." She could barely get the words out. Talking required thinking, and her mind had turned to mush. Her nipples were points of need. Her crotch throbbed. Her entire body turned molten with craving.

Without warning, he closed his mouth over her clit, sucking hard. Somehow, one of his hands was between her legs with fingers inside, thrusting and touching her sensitive places. She laced her fingers into his hair, holding his head in place.

He let go of her clit and ran his tongue around it. Up one side, down the other, another swirl, and then more sucking. She mewled with delight as heat swamped her, lust and hunger spilling from every point of contact and traveling to all the nerves in her body.

It was as if he was perfectly attuned to her arousal. He brought her almost to the point of release, backed off, and did it again. She gave in, turned everything over to him. Eyes closed, head thrown back, she became a slave to sensation and the giddy delight cascading through her.

He let go abruptly, slid from beneath the grip she had on his head. Her eyes snapped open. Before she could ask why he'd stopped, he swung her legs onto the bed and knelt between them, a hand wrapped around his cock.

His eyes glowing like exotic jewels, he pushed her legs wider. She wrapped them around his waist, and he seated himself at the entrance to her vault. His nipples had formed hard peaks too, their coppery surfaces puckered into points of desire.

She wriggled, anxious to draw him inside. He went slow, letting her accommodate and stretch to fit him. Before settling them on her hips, he ran his hands down her body.

"You have no idea how incredible you feel." He twitched his cock where he'd buried it within her.

She tightened her muscles around him. "Maybe

not, but I know how good you feel. Now, move, goddammit."

"I like a woman who knows what she wants."

"Good, because right now I want you."

He grinned down at her. "I won't last long. But just wait until round two."

She thrust upward, and he withdrew just as slowly as he'd entered her. The second stroke was equally deliberate. And the third. She cupped her breasts, rubbing the nipples.

He made that wonderful male sound again, the one that let her know how much he ached for her, and then he moved faster. No longer titrating anything, he drove into her quick and sure. She tightened her grip around his waist, tilting her pelvis so every stroke caught her clit. Heat surrounded her, drove her higher and higher still. She was pinching her nipples now, wringing every last drop of reaction from her body.

He swept both her arms above her head, pinning them effortlessly in place as he continued to fuck her. Bending his head, he slashed his mouth over hers. Panting and gasping, they ground their bodies together, driving one another onward. A climax rolled through her, followed almost immediately by a second one as he came. The judders of his orgasm and the splashes of semen toppled her over the crest again.

He let go of her wrists and sank down onto her,

breathing hard. She wrapped her arms around him, holding tight as their bodies quieted.

He was still buried inside her, still hard. "That was wonderful," she murmured against his chest. "Thank you."

He turned them onto their sides, cock still inside her, and positioned himself so he could look at her. "If we're into thanking, it's me who should be thanking you, but this wasn't just sex. I want you to become part of my life. Forever. We've entered precarious times, but I'm falling in love with you. It's a gift from the goddess, and I'd be worse than a fool to spurn it. Or put it off until we enter gentler waters."

Shock vied with delight. "But we don't know each other well enough."

"You're stuck in modern times. Think back to our roots, sweetheart. How long did it take to find a mate a few hundred years ago?"

"But those matings were arranged, by our families."

"So?" He quirked a blond brow. "Instead of telling me why we won't work, tell me why we will."

He was so earnest and so engaging, it made her smile.

"*Tell him,*" her eagle urged.

"I heard that," Jeremiah said. "Tell me what?"

Heat rose to her face, making her rosier than she already was from her climaxes. She caught her lower lip between her teeth. "I don't know how much stock you put in astrology, but Sarai had a few ideas about us. So did one of her lore books."

"Really?" The eyebrow edged higher. "Like what?"

"According to her, our mating is foretold—in the stars."

A thoughtful smile crossed his face, making him look like an old-world scholar. "No wonder I was so attracted to you. I couldn't figure it out, but it all makes perfect sense now."

"I'm glad someone believes in psychic mumbo-jumbo."

"You don't?"

She laughed. "Your next question is going to be why someone magical doesn't believe in psychic phenomena. I put stock in most of them, but astrology never did much for me. My eagle's given me a raft of shit over the years because of it."

"Philosophy aside"—he ran gentle fingers over her cheek—"will you share my life? I'll do everything in my power to protect you, see you want for nothing."

The eagle crowed, shrieked, cawed, and then repeated itself.

"Your bird just said yes," Jeremiah noted. "How about you?"

She'd always been cautious, testing waters before entering them.

And look where it's gotten me. A long, lonely life where I'm mostly alone unless I'm at work.

In a burst of spontaneity, she tilted her chin, kissed him once, and said, "Yes, but with the caveat I've lived alone forever, and I can be a bitch on wheels."

He rolled his eyes. "Yeah. I've seen that part. If it's the worst you throw my way, we're golden."

She kissed him again. Cradling her head, he kissed her back. She'd been planning to get up, but when he urged her mouth to open with his tongue and flexed his cock, still encased in her body, she abandoned her agenda.

He broke their kiss long enough to say, "Tell me how you want us to be. Last time was my choice. This time is yours."

"I was thinking about getting up. It must be close to dawn."

He angled his head to one side. "Is that what you really want?"

She shook her head. "Nope. I want you. We could stay in this bed until we starved to death, and I'd die a happy woman."

"Music to my ears, darling. We can call for takeout. Or the others can. Or Chloe and Stella can cook something. They're the resident kitchen wizards."

"Stella?"

"The redhead with blonde streaks. She's mated to

Raul. You'll get everyone straight, but right now it's a pretty low priority."

She hip-butted him until she was on top. "How about like this? And then we'll get up and let everyone know about us."

He nuzzled her neck. "Renee, sweetheart, this house is filled with magic-wielders. It's a sure bet they already do."

She laughed again, not remembering when she'd laughed this much maybe ever. "You've turned my brain to pudding."

He twitched his cock, moving slightly in and out. "So long as my trusty appendage doesn't join it, all is well."

She snugged her body around him, delighted by the feel of him, the smell of him, and the rightness of him inside her. Maybe there was more to astrology—and the lore books—than she realized. She'd have to tell Sarai, but later, much later.

Jeremiah drew her against him and kissed her. She kissed him back, welcoming the sexual heat as it enveloped them transporting her to another plane.

A Week Later

Jeremiah was happy, happier than he remembered. Happier than anyone had a right to be, but he wasn't questioning any of it. The mate bond was in full bloom, and he and Renee caught up in newly mated bliss. His residual angst from killing his own people was fading, but some scars cut deep, and this one would never totally go away.

He halted his wanderings around the yard to smile. He'd done a whole lot of that lately. The wonder of discovering more about his mate had pushed the previous week's carnage to a manageable place. Not gone, but not haunting him, either.

He and Renee had made a few plans. Since she was the one with a job that required her presence in a specific place, he'd return to Montana at least long enough for her to work a few more months before giving notice. Eventually, they'd return to Colorado. It was a solid beginning, but he didn't actually believe things would slow down enough for them to put it into action.

Not anytime soon.

What was far more likely was they'd make a trip to Montana to clear out her house, but he hadn't given voice to that.

Renee longed for her old life, and keeping her happy was at the very top of his list. Building fantasies of the life they both wanted didn't hurt anything. It might not happen until next year or five years down the road, but eventually they had to reach an end to the vampire and mage problems.

He suspected many mages would make the same transition he had: the one to becoming a shifter. Once kicked open, the door was unlikely to close. Unfortunately, it would do nothing but exacerbate their problems with other mages...

The back door slammed, and Niall clattered down the steps, joining him in the backyard.

"Did they throw you out too?" Jeremiah asked.

"Sure and they did. What kind of bullshit separates a man from his mate? We never did that in the Old Country."

"You're not remembering. They always kept us

apart right before the mating ceremony. I'm surprised you and Sarai haven't already formalized your bond."

"Aye, and when would we have had the chance?" Niall retorted. "'Tis been one catastrophe after another. I didn't think we'd pull off tonight's festivities. I was certain—"

"Ssht." Jeremiah shook his head. "Bad luck to give voice to such thoughts." He'd been expecting a vampire attack too, but the fuckers had held off this long, so perhaps they'd have a few more hours of peace and quiet. Enough to complete the mating ritual that would bind him to Renee and Niall to Sarai.

"Probably right, mate." He slugged Jeremiah in the arm. "Congratulations, by the way. I never got a chance to tell you what a lucky bloke you are. Renee is one of the best. Just like Sarai."

"My cave lion said much the same thing."

A rumbly purr rolled from his mouth. The beast was back in residence, apparently fully recovered from its brush with vampire toxin.

"Settling into your new magical affiliation?" Niall arched a dark brow.

"Hasn't been all that much of a transition—after the first little bit when we weren't sure of one another."

Niall's pleasant expression shaded to one far more somber. "I haven't wanted to bring this up, but have any of you been in communication with your mage kin?"

"I've tried," Jeremiah admitted.

"No dice?"

"About the size of it." He blew out a tight breath. "Best I can figure is word travels fast, and everyone knows I led the charge that killed a whole lot of us."

Niall frowned. "But they'd sold out to evil."

"Maybe not all of them. We didn't take the time to find out. These types of things grow with the telling, but we did draw mage fire to murder mages as they lay shackled to the ground. It's not our way to kill our own."

"Aye, I remember. You were separating them from their magic as punishment." At Jeremiah's nod, he went on. "Wouldn't have worked. Not with what we faced."

Jeremiah raked a hand through his hair. His fingers snagged on decorative beadwork Chloe had worked into his short locks for the wedding, and he lowered his hand. "You know that. I know that. All of us who were there understand the way things were but communicating it to someone who didn't see what we did isn't easy."

"Damn near impossible if they've shut you out of their communication loop. Do you have a central governance of any type?"

"Nope. Not since we left the Old Country. Main reason for it there was to monitor how the war with you folks was going." He narrowed his eyes. "Do you have one?"

"Nay, but I'm trying to not leave any stone unturned. We have to open the communication channels. Every single mage is in danger. We spread the word through the shifter communities to be vigilant and warded. To take naught for granted."

"Do you think it odd we've been undisturbed since we left the cave?" Jeremiah drew his brows together.

"Aye. And nay. Vamps had come to count on an infusion of magic from their mage puppets. Absent that, they probably require time to regroup."

"Regroup, as in shanghai another passel of mages to strip mine for magic?"

Niall nodded. "I'm as sure as I've ever been of anything that is precisely what they're up to. When they come after us, they'll want to be at full power. Those cocky fuckers hate to lose, and they lost both manpower and pride."

Respect for his mate swelled through Jeremiah, but he sobered fast. She'd outsmarted four vampires with flattery—and blinded two more—which meant they'd be on the lookout for her.

He was ready for them. Him and the lion. Those

bloodsucking abominations wouldn't hurt Renee. Not on his watch.

"Almost ready, fellows," Chloe called from the back porch and vanished back inside.

"Apologies," Niall said. "Today is joyous. I shouldn't have sullied it with—"

"Reality?" Jeremiah inserted dryly. "We have work to do. Lots of it, but the brunt of our tasks can wait until after our matings are official. I have a few ideas we can run down later in the week."

"About locating other mages?"

"Yes. I know where several groups of us live in neighboring states. If they won't respond to telepathy, we'll have to show up in person."

Niall pushed a clump of dark hair out of his face. "How do you know they'll let you in or listen to you?"

Jeremiah snorted. "We're a polite lot. They may ask me to leave, but if I request a brief audience, they'll grant it."

"What makes you think they'll listen?"

"Because I can send them an image of what we encountered in the cave. They'll recognize vampire stench all over it." He linked an arm through Niall's. "No more of this right now. We're going to go inside, stand next to our mates, and pledge our hearts and souls to them."

"Before we do," Niall said, "Thanks for forgiving

me. I value you as a friend, and I don't say that to very many people."

"No hard feelings. That stunt I pulled with the poison was an act of desperation. I can see how you'd view me as a reckless cowboy with no regard for anyone else who got caught up in my craziness."

Niall snorted. "Reckless blackguard might be closer to the mark. Not many cowboys in Ireland."

Jeremiah chuckled and led the way inside, clearing his mind of everything but the upcoming festivities. He walked through the kitchen and into the front room and stopped dead. The high-ceilinged great room had been decorated with groups of fragrant lit tapers, evergreen boughs, and extravagant flower arrangements. They must have cost a fortune this time of year. Most of the old-fashioned furniture had been pushed against the walls, creating a large, open space. Like the rest of the house, this room had oak flooring covered with Oriental rugs.

People stood in small groups, chatting softly. A few called out greetings to him and Niall.

"What do you think?" Chloe trotted to his side beaming.

"It's beautiful."

She nodded. "I thought so too. For once, I ordered food from a catering company. It should be here in an hour or so."

"Who all is here, and is anyone else coming?"

"Bunches of shifters I don't know are already here, and more are arriving every few minutes. Stephan and Sarai did an excellent job with that part of things." She didn't mention that her efforts to invite their mage kin were met with silence, much as his attempts to communicate with them had been spurned.

He hugged his sister. "Thank you."

She held onto him for a long minute before letting go. "No need. It's not every day one of us finds a mate."

A wistful undercurrent in her voice tore at his heart. Some magic wielders married humans, but the pairings were always difficult. Knowing you'd go on the same while your partner aged and eventually died was a bitter pill. Other problems, like finding excuses for your perpetual youth, was another issue. Hiding evidence of your magic, yet a third.

"You'll find someone," he reassured her.

She shrugged and offered a stock answer. "If the goddess wills it."

Music swelled from the far end of the room. Raul and Mariel played a variety of instruments. This time mellow guitar strumming was joined by the high, pure notes of a flute.

The double doors leading to a morning room opened, and Renee and Sarai walked through. Both women wore long, flowing colorful gowns with golden circlets holding their hair back and bunches of fragrant roses and lilies in their arms, but Jeremiah had eyes only for Renee.

Her golden hair hung loose creating a shining cape that spilled to her waist. Her green eyes glowed with tenderness as she latched onto his gaze. He walked toward her, meeting her midway across the room, and opened his arms, intent on embracing her without crushing the bouquet.

"Couples front and center," Stephan boomed from in front of the fireplace. Flames crackled merrily. "I haven't performed a mating ceremony in centuries."

Renee slid her hand beneath his arm. "You look gorgeous. Too bad we can't run upstairs for a quickie."

"Hang onto that thought. The ceremony won't last forever."

"You don't know Stephan."

They walked slowly to the brick hearth that fanned out from the fireplace and took their pre-arranged spots. He and Renee were to the right. Niall and Sarai to the left.

Stephan nodded his approval and began chanting in Gaelic. Jeremiah's eyes widened. This was the old mating ritual. The original one from when they were still one people. He offered Stephan kudos for locating it. The Internet was a grand tool for a lot of things, but magical castings and rituals—the real ones anyway—weren't located in cyberspace.

"Repeat after me," Stephan intoned. "First Niall and Sarai, and then Jeremiah and Renee."

"Aye, we shall repeat your words," the four of them said in unison.

"And now we begin," Stephan intoned, pausing at intervals for them to recite each phrase.

"You cannot possess me for I belong to myself
   But while we both wish it, I give you that which is mine to give
   You cannot command me, for I am a free person
   But I shall serve you in those ways you require
   and the honeycomb will taste sweeter coming from my hand

I pledge to you that yours will be the name I cry aloud in the night and
   the eyes into which I smile in the morning
   I pledge to you the first bite of my meat and the first drink from my cup
   I pledge to you my living and my dying, each equally in your care
   I shall be a shield for your back and you for mine

I shall not slander you, nor you me

I shall honor you above all others, and when we quarrel we shall do so in

private and tell no strangers our grievances

*T*HIS IS *my wedding vow to you*

This is the marriage of equals."

"FOR THIS IS the marriage of equals," Renee said and raised eyes the color of uncut emeralds to gaze at Jeremiah. Her expression, tender and passionate, mixed into a blend uniquely hers and filled him with joy.

This was his woman. His. From now and forever more.

"Hold out your hands," Stephan instructed.

When they did, he made small incisions in the balls of their thumbs. None of them needed further details. Jeremiah pressed his wound to Renee's and let their blood flow together. Scribed by magic, the cut places began healing almost at once.

"It is done," Stephan said. "By the power vested in me by the goddess, Gaia, I solemnize your matings. Bring pride upon yourselves and your progeny. Be a shining beacon to heal the rift between our people."

Among a chorus of, "Congratulations," and "I'll drink to that," Jeremiah gathered Renee into his arms and kissed her.

She wrapped her arms around him and her scent, reminiscent of wildflowers and cinnamon, soothed and inflamed him by turns. His cock swelled, pressing into her belly, and he felt like he'd come home.

Someone tapped his shoulder, and Stephan said, "You've guests to meet, son. The two of you have all your long lives to make love."

Renee dragged her mouth from his long enough to glance at Stephan. "Killjoy."

Stephan laughed. "May you always be as happy and as entranced with Jeremiah as you are today. My Marie and I never lost our spark, so I know it's possible."

Jeremiah let go of Renee and extended his hand. Stephan grasped it. "Thank you for officiating, and for coming up with the perfect ceremony."

"You recognized it?" Stephan furled a blond brow.

"Of course. Any of us who've lived long enough would have."

"Over here," Sarai called. "We're starting a receiving line."

The doorbell rang; Chloe sprinted for it saying, "Food's here!" She pulled the door open, but instead of a catering company, a large group of mages strode inside and fanned out across the foyer.

Jeremiah's joy faltered. He told Renee, "Remain here."

"Bullcrap. Come on. Let's see what they want."

He wanted to protect Renee, keep her safe from harm, from ugliness, but it was her right as his mate to remain by his side if she chose. The words from their vows about honoring one another and a marriage of equals ran through his mind.

Chloe stood, hands on her hips, surveying the new arrivals. She glanced over one shoulder. "Jer?"

He loped across the room, Renee by his side, and faced his kinsmen, most of whom he recognized. "To what do I owe the pleasure of your presence?" He kept his words mild. As he'd told Niall, they were a polite people.

A medium-height mage with unruly brown hair, stubble-covered cheeks, and a burly build stepped forward. Leather leggings hugged his thighs, and a leather vest embossed with runes had been tossed atop a green woolen shirt. He trained keen dark eyes on Jeremiah.

"We heard about what happened," he began.

Jeremiah nodded. "Good to see you, Curt, even under these circumstances. Today is my wedding day. We tried to invite you and our other mage kin"—his gaze swept the group ranged behind Curt—"but you never responded to our telepathy."

"We heard you right enough," another mage, Curt's mate, Viva, joined him. As fair as he was dark, she wore a long black skirt topped by a multihued tunic.

Curt shot a pointed look her way, but she stared him down. "I've a right to speak my mind as well as you."

Curt cleared his throat. "Aye, but I'm the appointed spokesperson. We all agreed."

"Speak away." She rolled her eyes.

"We've known you since before coming to the States," Curt went on, aiming his message at Jeremiah. "None of us believed you capable of wholesale slaughter such as we heard about. Not without provocation."

He stopped to take a breath. Viva jumped into the breach and said, "So we decided to show up and talk with you direct like, find out what happened from the horse's mouth."

Curt tried to look indignant, but it was clear how fond he was of his mate.

"I'm grateful for the opportunity." Jeremiah bowed slightly.

The doorbell chimed again. Chloe wove around the mages and opened the door. This time, it was the catering company, and she ushered them inside, pointing the way to the dining room.

"It's our wedding day," Renee repeated what Jeremiah had said. "So long as you're here, please share our joy and break bread with us. We'll talk better with full bellies."

"Wedding day, you say?" A tall, thin mage strode forward from where he stood near the door. "Who officiated?"

"I did." Stephan extended a hand. "Stephan Lurie, and I'm most pleased to meet you."

"Alexander Westerly." The mage shook Stephan's hand. When he let go, he turned to face Jeremiah and Rene. "I offer my blessings and congratulations."

"Sure and we'll take some too." Niall and Sarai bounded forward.

Alexander's gaunt face split into a grin. "A double mating. Now there's truly reason for celebration. Blessings to you as well."

Jeremiah released the breath he'd been holding. He'd expected Alexander, their de facto cleric, to pitch nine kinds of fits he hadn't been the one to conduct the ceremony. Never mind he hadn't responded to telepathic efforts to reach him. And a few cell phone calls as well.

Renee clapped her hands together, her smile so radiant it could have lit universes. "Grand. It's settled.

Come and eat. We'll send that catering service back to make more if we need to."

She gestured to the mages and shifters scattered through the room. Grabbing Jeremiah's hand, she set a direct course for the dining room.

Lost in a whirlwind of introductions, hearty good wishes, backslaps, and toasts as the afternoon turned to evening, Jeremiah reminded himself he'd always been a lucky man. That the mages had sought him out was a good sign. They had a whole lot of talking to get through—and the matter of his cave lion bondmate—but he'd take it one step at a time.

The most important thing was Renee. His wife. His mate. His love.

"You look happy." She handed him an overflowing plate.

"Set that down."

"Not hungry?" She laid the plate on a nearby table.

"Of course I am, but I'm a man with strong priorities, and right now my priority is you."

Drawing her into an embrace, he closed his mouth over hers. He'd never get enough of the feel of her, the taste of her, but he let her go and winked broadly.

She winked back, stabbed a particularly lush berry with a fork, and fed it to him. "Have I told you lately how much I love you?"

"Not for the last hour. Say it again. I love to hear it."

Her eyes gleamed, and she leaned close, another berry poised near his mouth. "I love you, heart of mine. Now and always."

"Now and always. I like the sound of that." He plucked the berry off the fork hovering in front of his mouth. It burst into a lush combination of sweet and tart on his tongue. She had another ready, but he pried the fork from her fingers and fed it to her.

"I love you, Renee. Thanks for taking a chance on us."

She started to laugh. "It wasn't much of a chance. Astrology and lore books are never wrong. Remember, a shifter's mate—"

"Is in the stars," he finished for her.

You've reached the end of *Lion's Lair*, book two of the Wylde Magick series. There's a lot of material to draw from in this world where vampires are on the offensive, draining magic—and blood—where they find it. Look for new Wylde Magick books through the end of 2018 and into 2019. Book three is already on the drawing board with an October release date. It's Chloe's story and a hero I have yet to create. All I know so far is he'll be a Libra.

Please, please leave a review for Lion's Lair. Do it now while you're thinking about it. It doesn't have to be fancy. A couple of sentences would be great. Thanks so very much.

If you enjoyed this book, you might like my Soul Dance series. Full-length alternate-history, urban fantasy featuring shifters, gypsies, and vampires. An excerpt from *Tarnished Legacy,* one of the Soul Dance books, follows.

ABOUT THE AUTHOR

Ann Gimpel is a USA Today bestselling author. A lifelong aficionado of the unusual, she began writing speculative fiction a few years ago. Since then her short fiction has appeared in several webzines and anthologies. Her longer books run the gamut from urban fantasy to paranormal romance. Once upon a time, she nurtured clients. Now she nurtures dark, gritty fantasy stories that push hard against reality. When she's not writing, she's in the backcountry getting down and dirty with her camera. She's published over sixty books to date, with several more planned for 2018 and beyond. A husband, grown children, grandchildren, and wolf hybrids round out her family.

Keep up with her at www.anngimpel.com or http://anngimpel.blogspot.com

If you enjoyed what you read, get in line for special offers and pre-release special reads. Newsletter Signup!

Germany, 1940

Half Romani, Tairin's no stranger to hiding her mixed blood from gypsy caravans. What she can't hide is her perpetual youth, courtesy of her shifter heritage. Every few years, she drops out of sight, resurfacing in a new country to join a caravan where no one knows her. She's overstayed her welcome where she is, but Germany is at war, and travel has become all but impossible for everyone targeted by the Reich.

Elliott's clairvoyance is strong, even for a Romani. Seer for all the caravans in Germany, he catches Tairin eavesdropping outside their leader's wagon one night. He should turn her in, but it would mean her execution, and he can't bring himself to do that. Instead, he interrogates her. Her magic is different, but he can't figure out quite what she is.

Any association between Romani and shifters is forbidden, and Tairin shields herself from Elliott's probing. She should leave right now, tonight. It would be easy enough. Shift to her wolf form and run, keeping out of hunters' gunsights. She's on the edge of flight when Elliott suggests a covert task to prove her loyalty. Tairin agrees immediately, kicking herself for being weak where he's concerned. Shifters and Romani have no future together. Zero. Zilch.

She should be smart about this and vanish into the night—before he discovers what she is and destroys her.

*J*anuary 1940
Munich, Germany

ELLIOTT BREND MOVED his hands in a circular pattern over three lit candles, the stench of wax made from sheep fat sharp in his nostrils. Patterns danced like mad creatures on the walls of his grotto, and he chanted faster to bring his casting to life.

Darkness swirled, surrounding him. The candles guttered and died, their wicks drowning in pools of grease. Elliott bolted to his feet, hands extended, still working the spell he'd summoned. Fear thickened his tongue, but he couldn't stop now. Partially cast spells would make it possible for the demon he'd apparently conjured to drag him back to Hell with it. Usually this casting brought visions, not an actual entity.

The temperature in the grotto plummeted until ice crystals formed in the air. Wind wailed, thin and menacing, until shudders racked him.

"Why have you freed me? Not that I'm complaining, mind you." The words echoed around Elliott, chilling him further. "Speak, human. While you still can."

Elliott tried. Instead of words, a breathy croak emerged. He swallowed around his dry-as-dust throat. "F-future," he stammered. "What will happen? Many of the Rom have been captured."

Unholy laughter drove into Elliott's brain like overheated nails. It took all his self-control not to clap his hands over his ears, but if he did that, he'd be lost. His spell would falter, as would his tenuous hold on the demon. He'd be damned if he'd cede the upper hand to it.

Who am I kidding? It already has all the power it needs.

"You scarcely require me for future-telling," the disembodied voice said. At least the profane laughter had stopped. After the briefest pause, it added, "Flee while you can. Or the Rom will die out—here and elsewhere."

"Why do you care?" The words tore out of Elliott before he could stop himself.

"About your people? I don't, but magical energy will keep me on this side of Hell. Along with death. Fear helps too." A low, menacing chuckle. "It's a perfect mix."

Elliott gathered power, letting it surge through him. The demon may have ridden in on the coattails of his earlier spell, but he couldn't allow it to remain. Too much evil was running unchecked as it was. Sparks crackled from his fingertips, burning him until his flesh smoked. The incantation, a surefire way to banish Hell's minions, crashed to the rotting wooden floor in a shower of glowing embers.

"Don't waste your magic, human."

"It's not a waste to return you to your proper place," Elliott snarled, wishing he could see the fucking thing.

"Try that last trick again, and you're a dead man."

Elliott sucked in a frustrated breath. He'd suspected the Rom were in serious danger. Signs they'd soon be targeted *en masse*, right along with the Jews, were impossible to ignore. All he'd sought this night was corroboration—and now he had it. He changed the cadence and timbre of his chant, hoping for an end to his spell, the hideous cold, and the abomination that scared the shit out of him. All he wanted now was for it to leave since returning it to Hell was beyond his ability.

"I am not leaving yet," the voice informed him. "You have no power over me, but you've already figured that out. Evil has risen. Rampant. Ubiquitous. As I noted earlier, it feeds me, right along with your magic."

Elliott clamped his jaws together to stop his teeth from chattering. What had he loosed on the world? "You must return at some point." He infused compulsion into his words. "If not today, or tomorrow, then surely soon. The dynamic balance between worlds will fail if you remain on Earth."

Laughter again. This time, it was even more loathsome and obnoxious.

"You haven't been paying attention, *human*. That dynamic balance? It's on its way out." Still laughing, the thing's foul presence receded.

Elliott sank into a crouch, mostly because his legs shook too badly to hold him upright. He wrapped his arms around himself and rekindled the candles with a jot of magic, welcoming their pools of light. Because it was easier than reconstructing what just happened— and the wickedness now free because of him—he shuffled through options.

The demon's advice—if demons even handed out such things—had been to flee. But where? Austria,

Poland, and Czechoslovakia were out of the question. Austria was a German ally. Both Poland and Czechoslovakia had fallen to German occupation a few months earlier. France would soon be under German rule. While his seer skills weren't absolute, he'd seen that particular event clearly.

Even if they could find a favorable location, how would they move the entire Romani population of Germany? They still favored wagons, so any kind of stealth exodus was out of the question.

He rose to his feet and shambled to a window, gazing out at a moonless night. The elders from all the Rom groups in Germany had assembled a few days earlier, and they were waiting for him to return. Though they dealt in magic, his particular affinity for the darker side of the spirit world unnerved many of his kin.

Should he confess what he'd done?

He'd loosed wickedness eager to sign on with the blood-soaked Nazi regime, but how much worse could things get? He knew what the work camps really were, and so did the other Rom. None of his people fit the Aryan model of perfection, and their nomadic lifestyle was an affront to neat rows of impeccable houses where blonde wives raised blonde children in perfect obedience to the Reich's precepts.

Not much leeway for the Roms' brightly colored

wagons or their sturdy horses. Their children who didn't go to school, or the canvas tents where they revealed futures, healed the sick, and fixed whatever was broken.

Bile splashed the back of his throat; he swallowed it down, and it burned all the way to his knotted belly. He still didn't understand how the Reich had mired Germany in such a chokehold, but it didn't matter. What did was ensuring Rom magic survived. It may have provided fodder for the newly released demon, but it also ensured the natural world would continue.

The traveling folk were tied to the world's beginnings in ways that had faded out of time and memory. They'd been run out of countries before and always endured, retooling themselves and keeping their magic under wraps as the world grew more modern.

If leaving Germany were impossible, they'd have to find a way to conceal themselves. The more he thought about it, the more the idea appealed to him. They faced evil, the likes of which the world had never seen. Evil that believed it could kill whomever it wished under the guise of cleansing the gene pool and producing a master race.

It would take gargantuan effort, but he and his kin could leverage magic to sabotage the Reich. Maybe even free the poor sods in those abominable camps.

And make damn good and sure Germany went down in flames it would never recover from. Elliott had no idea if the elders would agree, but he'd float his idea. See if their philosophy, *Opré Roma*—Roma arise—was more than empty words.

Even if they don't agree, there's nothing that says I can't gather a few handpicked companions...

He curved his hands into fists until his nails cut into his palms. The more he rolled it around in his mind, the better he liked the idea of small vigilante groups that struck fast and hard, while remaining invisible to the *SchutzStaffel*, Germany's elite corps of political soldiers.

Determination straightened his spine. He dug a warm cloak out of the clothing chest leaning against one wall and wrapped it around himself before striding out of his well-hidden grotto located beneath the city. Part of a deteriorating tunnel system under a crumbling castle, his hideaway dated back to Roman times. He'd titrate what he told the elders until he saw which way the wind blew. Once he had a sense of that, he could make better plans.

Tairin Jabari prowled from one end of a clearing to the other in a forested glen. Her Rom family group had established a temporary camp here after local authorities ousted them from their previous location inside Munich's city limits. A dozen wagons fanned out in a circle, and horses were hobbled off to one side where grass grew thickly. Cars might be faster, but the smoky, noisy contraptions that always required repair had never appealed to Romani sensibilities.

She rolled her shoulders back to quell the creature sharing her skin. Her wolf wanted out, but it was too dangerous. For all their magic, power they scattered about like so much faerie dust, the Romani were superstitious about shapeshifters.

Worse than superstitious. They hated them.

She pulled her thick, black wool cloak tighter around herself and buried her hands in its thick folds. Her leather boots were soaked through, but it was winter. Short days and wet ground meant they never dried completely. Reaching within, she soothed her wolf, agreed its lush double coat and furred paws were far better suited to damp and cold than their current arrangement.

"Promise me," the wolf spoke into her mind.

"Anything, heart of mine."

"Find us an hour where I can run."

Tairin closed her teeth over her lower lip, not wanting false words to fall between her and her bondmate. *"I'll do my best."* Whether *her best* would yield the privacy required remained to be seen.

Something mollified the wolf. Maybe her words. Maybe her honesty. It withdrew to the place where it lived when it wasn't front and center in her mind.

She'd managed to hide what she was from the group she traveled with for the better part of twenty years. Soon it would be time to fade away—to find another country and maybe more Romani traveling companions. As it was, several of the women had made snippy comments about her perpetual youth. Tairin led them to believe she employed a glamour, but no one had the kind of magic to keep something like that going all day, every day, for years.

The sounds of male laughter, boasts, and glasses slapping a tabletop rose from the leader's wagon. He played host to eleven other elders this week. They'd gathered to discuss the evil that had descended on Germany. Elliott, the group's seer, was off doing goddess only knew what. Maybe he'd actually have a vision that would galvanize the Rom into something beyond business as usual.

Not a moment too soon, her inner voice muttered sourly.

If the disaster she suspected were imminent fell out the sky and onto their heads, they'd be rounded up. Herded into the death camps sprouting like cancers across what used to be the Prussian empire.

And that would be that.

She'd find a way through. Her wolf form would see to it. She could join one of many packs that howled their way through Germany's thick forests. But she'd become fond of the Romani. That and shared blood was why she'd traveled with several of their family groups for the past hundred years.

She wove her way into a thick evergreen grove where she wouldn't have to hide the anger that still raked her whenever she remembered how her people had kicked her out. Looking back was a dead end, yet once she'd begun, it took time to redirect her energy.

She was different from other shifters. And other

Romani. Born of a forbidden coupling between a wolf shifter father and a Romani mother, she hadn't been welcome in either camp once her powers blossomed. Her moon blood presaged her first shift. That she could shift at will from a seemingly bottomless magical well sealed her fate with her shifter kin. They might have had more tolerance for how strong her magic was if her blood were pure, but it wasn't.

That she could shift at all meant the Rom wanted nothing to do with her.

Tairin took to her wolf form after that, and lived with local packs in northern India for her first hundred years, give or take a few. Some alphas accepted her; others drove her away. She'd been between packs when a caravan of Romani wagons passing through attracted her attention, alerted her it was time to be human again. As a wolf, she was used to following her instincts without overthinking things. After so long, her animal nature was firmly entrenched.

So firmly entrenched, her first shift back to her human body took days to finesse. A Romani fortuneteller with Runic markings on her face and hands had found Tairin with her arms wrapped around her naked body, crying. They didn't speak the same language, so she'd had a ready excuse not to reveal that her tears were relief she still had a human form. Over the days she'd languished part wolf, part human, she'd been petrified she'd never find the purity of either body again.

The woman who rescued her moved her into the back of her wagon. As Tairin regained her very rusty ability to speak, she discovered the Romani group was on the move, traveling through Pakistan, Persia, and Turkey on their way to Romania. The journey was hard and took years. She'd stuck with them throughout, helping as she grew stronger. Though her new family wanted to know all about her, the only part she'd revealed was that she had some Romani blood.

She'd never repeated her past mistake about spending years in a single form. Nor did she assume her adoptive tribe would be tolerant if they knew what she truly was, so she dove headfirst into learning Romani magic, never expecting to have an affinity for it.

Tairin smiled wryly at how wrong she'd been. In the end, she'd hidden just how potent her power was, so no one would guess she was anything other than Romani and human. And she'd waited for the unknown to rise to swallow her whole. Surely there was a reason the Rom avoided shifters. A reason why sexual congress was forbidden. Would her use of Romani magic leave her open to some hideous consequences?

Though she'd asked that question and others,

taking care to be subtle about it, no answers were forthcoming. The lore books were written in Coptic, an old Egyptian language no one in her caravan seemed to have mastered at anything beyond a cursory level. Tairin never learned to read very well as a child, so translation was beyond her skill level. She'd rectified being mostly illiterate, but her grasp of German and French didn't help to decipher the lore books.

She stifled a frustrated sigh. Her current group of companions was the fourth one she'd joined since leaving India. Given the rise of the Reich, it might well be the last.

The sounds of a horse galloping hard drew her back to the circle of wagons. Was Elliott returning? Or was an elder late to the party? She'd thought all were present and accounted for, but she might've been wrong. Tairin sent a slender thread of seeking magic outward. Elliott's energy resonated, making her heart flutter oddly.

The tall, broad-shouldered Rom with his long black hair and deep blue eyes moved with the grace of a large, jungle cat. Seer power ran strong in him, and he dabbled in the darker side of Rom magic. Enchantments from Black Magick came easily to her, but she hid that particular ability from her fellows.

Sometimes she'd caught Elliott's gaze on her,

sharply speculative. But if he saw through to what she was, he'd never said as much.

Elliott reined his horse to an abrupt halt, its thick hooves churning up clods of mud and stones. "Tairin." His voice rang with command and a surfeit of magic as he dismounted. "See to my horse." He tossed the reins her way and loped toward the wagon where the men held court. His leggy gait drew her gaze. He was so sensual, her body vibrated with wanting to throw herself into his arms. She'd never lain with a man, only with wolves, but she could imagine what it would be like.

Maybe it's time.

Maybe not. I got away with learning Rom magic. I might not be so lucky making love with one.

How would her half-breed blood react to joining with a Romani? She couldn't ask the question without giving away far too much about who she was.

She plucked the reins out of the dirt and sent soothing energy directly into the horse's mind. The stallion had been ridden hard. He needed a cool down, so she vaulted onto his back and walked him at a sedate pace until he stopped tossing his head and his breathing slowed. Some horses sensed her dual nature and resented the hell out of it, but the stallion seemed oblivious.

She'd tethered him near his fellows where he could

graze and removed his saddle and bridle before curiosity drew her to the wagon where men's voices droned. Someone had shielded the conversation unfolding within, but she cut through the barrier with ease. Hunkering a few feet away, she eavesdropped shamelessly, wanting to know what would happen next.

Women fared better with the traveling folk than they did elsewhere, but Romani society was still run by men. When she sent her power spiraling outward to listen in on the men, the other women were all in their wagons, probably pretending all was well. The men—beyond the elders—milled about, busy with myriad tasks that needed doing each night. Younger children remained with their mothers. Older boys and girls helped the men do chores. Normally, they'd have set up their tents and wagons in Munich, soliciting local business, but the resident police force had made it abundantly clear they were no longer welcome.

Tension thickened the air. Even though everyone was acting as if tonight was just one more winter evening, they all knew better. Decisions unfolding one thin wall away from her would bind them to a course that might well spell their doom. A hissing snort bubbled up; Tairin smothered it fast before one of the elders heard and came out to investigate.

She swathed herself in invisibility and tilted her head, listening intently.

"You loosed a demon?" Michael thundered.

"How could you have been so irresponsible?" another voice she didn't recognize broke in.

"It's not as if that was my intent." Elliott's even baritone held a calming element. "I cast a scrying spell seeking visions, not one of Hell's minions." He paused for a few seconds, probably to strengthen the spell that lay beneath his words. "I did my damnedest to send the bastard packing. I wasn't strong enough, but we waste time speaking of him. We must decide how to proceed."

"Ye say the demon advised flight?" Stewart's Scottish brogue was unmistakable.

"Yes," Elliott replied.

"When we begin believing anything that emerges from a demon's mouth, we're finished," Michael said flatly.

"Och aye. Still, we canna remain here," Stewart said. "We canna work. We've been banned from the town."

"It won't be any different in Berlin or Heidelberg or Dresden," Elliott said. "The Reich have labeled our kind as undesirables. Our way of life is anathema to them."

"And ye know what happens next." Stewart's

words sounded like a dirge. "We join the others. The ones imprisoned by those Nazi bastards."

"Let me say my piece," Elliott cut in. "Then you can decide what's best for your individual groups."

"I'm not certain I want to listen to someone who let a demon loose to feed off the poison spreading across Europe," another elder grumbled.

"Your choice." Elliott spoke clearly, but without inflection. "My path is clear."

"Really?" Michael's single word dripped displeasure. "Last time I checked, you were part of my group, which means you're bound by my decisions."

Elliott cleared his throat. "Nowhere is it written that you own me, nor that I signed on with you for life. Look, men, we have a problem. If we continue to ignore it, the Nazis may well add us to their genocide list—"

"They already have," Stewart broke in. "I, for one, would like to hear what the lad has to say. Listening doesna bind us to action."

"Fine," Michael muttered dourly. "Proceed, but make it quick."

After a period of silence where Tairin held her breath, Elliott began to speak again. "Very well. Escape from Germany is unlikely, not in our numbers. A few of us might get lucky, but most of us will end up trapped. Neighboring countries aren't a haven. Either they're already occupied, or they soon will be." He inhaled noisily and blew it out. "Our only option as I see it is to hide. If we remain in our groups, they're manageable enough we might be able to pull it off."

"What aren't you saying?" Michael demanded. "I damn near raised you, Elliott. I know when there's more than what's come out of your mouth."

"I'm impressed." Elliott laughed softly. "You do know me, probably far too well. I plan to leverage my magic and do what I can to sabotage the Reich. I'm not certain how it will play out, but if I strike fast and hard, I can catch them off balance. By combining my seer ability and maybe astral projection or invisibility spells, I should be able to determine where my efforts will create the most damage."

"So will ye be doing this on your own, lad?" Stewart asked.

"If need be, yes," Elliott replied. "I admit, it would be better if a small group of us signed on, but this will be extremely dangerous, and I won't ask anyone else to risk discovery—and maybe death—if things go wrong."

"You might have discussed this with me first." Michael's tone held censure.

"When would I have had a chance?" Elliott shot back. "This idea only took shape today, after the demon left me to stew in my own guilt for having offered it free passage from Hell."

"Mmph. The way I see it," Michael said, "we have three choices. Business as usual. Attempt to make our way to somewhere the Nazi scourge hasn't touched. Or conceal our presence."

"That was my assessment," Elliott murmured.

"Ye did well, lad," Stewart said. "Now leave us so we may determine if we all bet on the same nag, or if we separate our fortunes."

Tairin had crept so close, she leaned against one of the wagon's wheels. The sound of scuffling footsteps as Elliott exited the wagon happened fast. Too fast for her to scamper into the forest. Barely breathing, she wound another layer of spells around herself, hoping invisibility would hide her presence. Once Elliott retired to the wagon he shared with three other unattached men, she could make her way to her own bedroll in one of the women's wagons.

Elliott trotted by where she crouched. He moved fast enough, she let herself hope she'd avoided discovery. Listening in on the elders, particularly after they'd shielded their conversation against prying ears, would surely earn her a session with the bullwhip. If not worse.

For long, tense moments, she thought she'd pulled it off. She was just starting to breathe again when Elliott's heavy tread first slowed and then stopped.

Shit! Crap!

"Become me," her wolf piped up. *"We can knock him down and be gone before he knows what hit him."*

"We can't shift that fast."

Magic, shockingly strong, probed her perimeter. The gig was up. Elliott might not know it was her, but he realized something was next to Michael's wagon. Something that had no business there.

More power pushed against her invisibility spell, growing in intensity until he punched through. His magic ceased abruptly.

"Tairin!" ricocheted through her brain. *"I know it's you. Don't bother denying it. Get over here. Now."*

She rose to her feet, letting go of her spell as she moved to where he stood twenty yards away. She'd be damned if she'd cower, so she straightened her shoulders and stared him right in the eyes.

"Follow me," he ground out.

"Why should I?" she countered.

He spoke into her mind. *"You have two choices. Either I call Michael, tell him what you were about, and let him decide what to do with you."*

"Or?" She feigned bravado she was far from feeling.

"We go someplace more private, and you tell me what the hell you were doing listening in on the elders' discussion." He narrowed his eyes to slits, but switched to speaking aloud. "I might still have to tell Michael.

Just so we're clear about that. I owe him allegiance. As do you."

Tairin jerked her chin toward thick timber. "Lead out."

Elliott shook his head. "Nope. You first. I'll be right behind you. And I warn you, if you try anything, I'll flatten you with magic and ask questions later."

She made her way to the grove of pines and firs where she'd been earlier. It was staring to drizzle, so she pulled her hood over her head. Tairin took her time as she worked on organizing which blend of truth might fly better. He'd be able to sniff out falsehoods right away.

His energy pounded against her back as she retraced her steps from earlier. She picked out anger, disbelief, and oddly enough, disappointment. Where was that coming from?

Tairin ducked beneath a low hanging limb and turned to face Elliott. It was dark, but her shifter blood meant she saw quite well in low light conditions. Elliott's dark brows were drawn into a thick, disapproving line.

"Talk and talk fast, sister."

The sizzle of power surrounded her, and she recognized a truth casting. "Was that really necessary?"

"What do you think?" His voice was low, tight

with something she couldn't interpret. "I find you swaddled in invisibility spells right outside Michael's wagon. You were obviously listening in. I want to know why."

"That's fair." She let go of her earlier intention of weaving a tale about idle curiosity mixed with boredom. Opening her eyes wide, she netted him with her gaze, trying her hardest not to pay attention to his high forehead, square jaw, and thick, curly hair that almost begged her to sink her hands into it.

"Come on, Tairin." He sounded exasperated. "Talk or you won't leave me any choices. What are you? A Nazi spy?"

Her mouth dropped open. "Awk. Jesus Christ! Oh, hell no." She bristled. "I have eyes and ears. I see what's going on about us. If you must have the truth, I was thinking about leaving, setting out on my own because I could hide myself better that way."

The edges of his magic probed her again. Along with it, his scent rose, tickling her nostrils with bay rum and piquant vanilla. She couldn't help herself, she breathed deep, inhaling the maleness of him.

His power jabbed her when he delved deeper. She rubbed her forehead. "Ouch. Surely that's more than enough. You must've picked up truth in my words."

"I did." Without warning, he closed the distance between them and clasped her head between his hands, pushing her hood back onto her shoulders. Rain pounded from the sky, soaking her quickly.

The intense nearness of him made her knees weak, but she struggled, trying to get away. In all her years with the Rom, the only one who'd touched her had been that first fortuneteller, and the woman had a kind heart. She hadn't suspected a thing, and her touch was aimed at healing, not peeling back the layers of a secret Tairin had guarded for years.

"Stop!" She writhed in his grip.

His scent intensified, and the air around them turned silvery, glistening against the raindrops. Before he could dig deep enough to discover what she was, she wrapped her arms around his neck and pulled his mouth atop hers. The touch of his lips set fire to her blood, and she tightened her hold on him, kissing him as if the fate of the world rested on never letting go. Desire hot enough to set her heart racing sent sensation spilling through her.

After the briefest of hesitations, he buried his hands in her hair and sank his tongue inside her mouth. Something about the way he fell headlong into her embrace made her suspect he'd imagined kissing her just like this.

Whatever works. If this keeps him from unraveling my secrets, it's a small price to pay.

But she was deluding herself. She couldn't make

love with him without telling him what she was. He'd never forgive her. More importantly, she'd never forgive herself.

His cock swelled against her belly, rigid with need. What would he look like? Taste like? She ached to wrap a hand around that hardness and drag him inside her body.

Reluctantly, she tore her mouth from his and let go of him. "Sorry," she managed through panting breaths. "I don't know what got into me." She stole a quick glance upward through lowered lids before adding, "I— I'm a maiden. Not a harlot."

"I know." His voice heaved with yearning. "But you're right that this isn't a good idea. Not with all the problems we face."

She wasn't sure whether to agree, so she held onto a wary silence. Where would this go next?

He let go of her head. "Your magic is strong. As strong as any Rom I've ever come across. Yet you're not full blood."

She licked at her swollen lips, anxious to change the subject of her power. "I could help you."

"With what?"

She rotated one hand in a circle. "That plan you described. My magic is potent, and it would complement yours since I'm female."

"Hold on." He shook his head. "I was trolling for men. Women don't go to war."

"The hell they don't." She shook wet hair out of her eyes. Annoyance scoured her nerves, and she stuck out her chin. "Try me. If I don't pass muster, I'll either join the women and sew doilies, or more likely, I'll slip away and wage my own mutiny against the Reich."

His chiseled lips, lips she was having a hell of a hard time resisting, twitched into a smile. "You're on, woman. Feel like a ride?"

"Where are we going?"

"Somewhere we can plan our first offensive."